I0556754

Prairie Winds

Pandemonium

Masters of the Prairie Winds Club

Book Fourteen

by Avery Gale®

© Copyright June 2023 by Avery Gale
ISBN 978-1-954904-01-9

All rights reserved.
Cover Design by Dar Albert at Wicked Smart Designs
Editing by Sandy Ebel at Personal Touch Editing
Proofreading by Karen Bailey
Published by Avery Gale Books

Chapter One

Lilly

"DAMN. CAN YOU believe this? After all these years, they finally made pot legal." Tabby Lawrence blew a puff of smoke into the air and giggled. Staring into the distance, she sighed. Lilly smiled at her friend and envied the contentment floating around her longtime friend. Leaning back in her chair, Tabby appeared completely at ease before she added, "I didn't think those puckered asses in the statehouse would ever vote for recreational use, and I damned well didn't expect your honey to sign off on it."

Tabby's eyes were hidden behind her dark glasses, but Lilly West knew her well enough to recognize the amusement in her voice. The comment was directed at their mutual friend, Charlotte Benson. Charlotte's husband had married well... very well. Charlotte was a beautiful and brilliant heiress. Her family's financial backing was the only reason the man was in the statehouse.

Ordinarily, the small group of close friends took turns hosting their monthly margarita parties. Their homes offered the privacy the group needed to speak freely. They'd made an exception this time after Tobi and Gracie promised a sneak peek into the Prairie Winds Club's revamped Forum Shops. The specialty shops—which had been the brainchild of Lilly's daughter-in-law and her best

1

friend—were an overwhelming success. The shops catered to every conceivable kink. The concept was so successful, Tobi and Gracie spent several years replicating their business model at clubs around the country.

Lilly hadn't been surprised when her sons eventually tired of their wife being gone more than she was home. Gracie's husbands agreed, and since the women had been closing in on exhaustion, they'd agreed to transition to working remotely. Now that their children were away at school, Tobi and Gracie were starting to travel again. They'd spent the past few weeks updating the shops at Prairie Winds and expanding the domestically manufactured and handmade specialties.

Lilly was pulled back to the moment when the woman sitting beside her groaned.

"I didn't think I'd live to see this day, either, but let's face it, the old fart only capitulated because he's taxing the hell out of every leaf sold. I swear he'd dig up his poor, dead mama if he thought he could pry another couple of nickels from her cold, clenched fist. That woman was as tight as bark on a tree." Charlotte Benson rolled her intense blue eyes, grimacing at the thought of what her husband would do for money. His mother had been the most selfish woman Lilly had ever met. Millie Benson never met a charity she didn't disdain. Lilly knew Charlotte's college friends had been surprised when she married her politically motivated, on-again, off-again college sweetheart. Lilly suspected Charlotte was getting something from the relationship none of them understood, but she'd never unraveled the mystery.

Charlotte's parents and Lilly's in-laws had been friends since their children were young. Lilly had once asked her husbands why the stunner had married the uptight lawyer, but they'd shaken their heads and told her to leave it alone. Del's and Dean's refusal to explain only added fuel to the flame of her curiosity.

"You're probably right. Hell, if anyone would know, it would be you." Lilly leaned forward, taking a slow drink from the frosted margarita sitting in front of her. "There's a reason this concoction comes in a glass known as a fishbowl. I swear the goal is to freeze enough brain cells that you're incapable of minding your own business." Pressing her fingers against the bridge of her nose in a futile attempt to stave off the stabbing pain of brain freeze, Lilly groaned at the discomfort. "Damn, I'm turning into a lightweight. This is embarrassing." Shaking her head, she focused her attention on Charlotte. Tequila was never Lilly's precursor to smart choices, and it didn't look like today would be any different. "Why did you marry him, anyway? He's so damned uptight, I bet dogs howl in three counties when he farts."

Tabby and Charlotte burst into a fit of giggles, and Lilly knew the same mental picture was flashing through all of their minds. It wasn't that Lilly disliked the man... but she saw through his thinly veiled motivation. The man was a politician to his core. His pretty wife had always seemed like a prop rather than a soulmate. Her substantial trust fund was an added bonus. The last Lilly knew, Charlotte was still funding his campaigns.

"Yeah, he's puckered pretty tight, but I'm good at helping him relax." Charlotte wiggled her perfectly shaped eyebrows, sending Tabby and Lilly into another fit of laughter. For all their obvious differences, maybe the two of them at least enjoyed a healthy physical relationship. Lilly hoped for Charlotte's sake the sex was good because nothing else about the man looked appealing. Charlotte looked around before asking, "Where's Tobi? I thought she and Gracie were planning to join us. I swear those two are going to meet themselves at the door someday and wonder why some old lady is waltzing in like she owns the damned place."

"Tobi and Gracie went to the airport to meet their men. They are hoping to meet the young woman the team rescued, but I'll bet you dollars to donuts they get stuck bringing my sons and their luggage." Lilly didn't think Kent or Kyle would take a chance letting their wife or her best friend pepper the young woman with a thousand and one questions before a plethora of government alphabet agencies had the opportunity to debrief her. Tobi's natural curiosity, coupled with the fact she'd never met a stranger, meant she would know every detail of the covert operation by the time they made the short drive from Austin's airport to Prairie Winds.

"I still think your sons are missing a huge opportunity with Tobi and Gracie. I've never met two more resourceful women. Give them fifteen minutes with a stranger, and they'll know every juicy detail about the person they were simply chatting with, as well as all their new friend's known associates."

Lilly nodded her head in agreement and laughed because Tabby wasn't wrong. There was no denying Tobi West was a force of nature. Gracie, on the other hand, was more adept at concealing her steamroller nature.

"Kent would agree with you. I think he sees Tobi's potential, but Kyle isn't going to risk her safety. He tries to cover up his concern by masking it as dominance, but I can see it in his eyes—he is terrified of losing her." Taking another drink, Lilly shuddered when the tart flavor of the drink hit her tastebuds. "I swear those two sons of mine are clones of their dads. There are moments I have to take a deep breath and pull myself back to the present."

"I still don't think it's fair you have two men, and nobody kicks up a fuss. Seriously, what the hell?" Tabby threw a crumbled napkin and shook her head. "Are we still on for our trip? I'm looking forward to getting away." Tabby had been badgering her friends for a girls' trip for months. Once Lilly and Charlotte agreed to go, several others asked to join, and the last Lilly heard, the group was so large, they were going to need a damned bus rather than a rental car once they landed in Costa Rica. The group size meant they needed a larger hotel. Damn, the whole thing was getting out of hand.

"Del and Dean swear it takes two of them to keep me in line, but that's bogus. I'm the most cooperative person I know." Lilly grinned when her friends choked on their drinks. *Serves them right.* Unless someone had personal experience with a polyamorous relationship, they didn't have a clue how challenging the lifestyle could be. Del and Dean were the loves of her life, but that didn't mean the two of them didn't regularly drive her to distraction. By the time Lilly brought herself back to the moment, Charlotte and Tabby were looking at her expectantly. "What?"

"You seem awfully distracted today. What's going on?" Tabitha Lawrence was one of the state's most successful real estate agents in Texas for a reason. The woman didn't miss even the smallest detail. She'd taken over her husband's failing business when he'd been diagnosed with Alzheimer's a few years ago. Lilly often wondered if success was her friend's way of escaping the relentless nightmare of watching the man she adored slip away faster than anyone predicted.

"I'm thinking of writing a book. I could write erotic

5

romance if I tried." Lilly had been toying with the idea for a long time, but the timing was never right... until now. "I could spin some wild yarns, y'all."

"You put *yarns* in a book or your marketing, and you'll be laughed out of the writing world. That word hasn't been in vogue for years, and I've heard the slang changes so rapidly, even the most prolific authors struggle to keep up."

"I'll be a trendsetter, you'll see. Language is so fluid it probably cycles back to older terms now and again. I'll be ahead of the curve—keeping history in front of the people, reminding them of days gone by and all that other politically correct nonsense." Lilly snickered at her own joke.

Looking around, Lilly admired the perfectly landscaped gardens and painted concrete terraces. She sighed, knowing none of her stories could include any reference to Prairie Winds. The club's strict rules regarding confidentiality prohibited members from acknowledging the club or other members outside the club itself.

"I've talked to friends who follow various authors. The stories they tell about how some authors treat their peers and their fans are terrifying. Don't get me wrong, there are some nice people who are willing to help new authors, but for the most part, the writing community is competitive as hell. Are you sure you want to deal with a ruthless group of writers?"

Lilly knew her friends were trying to protect her, but she'd already made up her mind. She'd already outlined a couple of stories and was looking forward to putting them together.

"What are your men going to say about you smoking weed?" Tabby elbowed Lilly, nearly toppling her out of her chair in the process. "I can't see Del having much of a sense of humor about… well, about much of anything, now that I think about it." Tabby waved her hand in the general direction of one of the many security cameras and grimaced. "I'll bet the guys in the control center send copies of our little soiree to your men and Governor Ass Whistler." The women burst into laughter just as Tobi and Gracie stepped around the privacy hedge.

"What on earth? You all are toasted." Tobi's blonde hair lay in pale yellow waves around her shoulders, her blue eyes dancing with amusement. "The guys are going to have a hissy fit when they get back,"—she pulled her phone from her pocket and grimaced—"in about two minutes." She'd barely gotten the words out when the distinctive sound of a helicopter moved closer.

"I thought you were bringing home a guest?" Charlotte leaned so far to the side, trying to see around Tobi and Gracie, she started to fall. Tabby wrapped her hand around her friend's wrist to keep her from sliding out of her chair.

"We got stuck driving the equipment truck. For the life of me, I can't figure out how they managed to snooker us." Tobi seemed lost in thought for a few seconds before shaking it off. "I have to admit there are a few perks to driving something bigger than my first apartment. People move out of your way when you are driving a panel truck."

"They move because you drive the blasted thing like it's a Formula One race car. I was driving your car and could barely keep up." Gracie stepped around Tobi and poured herself a drink before collapsing into a chair. "We beat the damned helicopter, for God's sake, Tobi. It was a nightmare trying to keep up with you. I have a sinking feeling you have pulled me into another one of your messes. If I find myself ass deep into an alligator pit again, I'm going with the Stockholm Syndrome defense."

"Yeah, because that's always worked so well in the past." Tobi took a drink from the frozen concoction Lilly handed her and sighed. "Why do you insist on overdramatizing everything? And I keep telling you, the expression is *ass deep in alligators*. There is no pit or pulling. Take notes or something, for heaven's sake." Tobi shook her head and grinned as she poured her second margarita. When she heard the rotors slowing, Tobi was back on her feet. "Let's go. We want to get your feedback on the new shops before the grinching starts."

Lilly looped her arm through Tobi's, the two of them leading the way. It didn't escape Lilly's attention that Tobi deliberately took the path leading away from the main courtyard. Smiling to herself, she couldn't help but wonder how long her darling daughter-in-law thought she could avoid the coming shitstorm.

"I can hear them grumbling from here. Tobi, I vow on everything holy, if you have gotten me into trouble, I'm going to tell them you made me sign on my mother's life that I would stay on your bumper. You have this crazy notion trouble is divided by the number of participants, but it never works out that way."

"It's perfectly logical. It's not my fault no one here got the memo." Tobi cast a mischievous grin over her shoulder at the others before tapping the gate's security code. Skirting around the side of the building, Lilly gasped when she noted the changes to the cobblestone street that served as the Forum Shops' main street.

"Oh my, this is amazing. The flower boxes and lanterns change the whole aesthetic. When you said you added shops, I assumed you'd replaced some you didn't think were doing as well. I had no idea you added buildings."

"That's just it, we didn't. All we did was reconfigure

the space. It wasn't easy, and we made the architect crazy, but in the end, it saved us a lot of money." Gracie was finally focused on showing the group the changes rather than worrying about what her husbands were going to say about their NASCAR-worthy trip back to Prairie Winds.

"And once we know it works, we'll be able to help others replicate our success." Tobi was bouncing on the balls of her feet, her excitement almost palatable. "So far, the shops at the other clubs have been so successful, they haven't been able to keep up with demand and have been asking for help to expand."

Gracie stepped forward, adding, "We also added a few new vendors as mobile carts. They'll remind you of beach vendors who can move from place to place. We want to know how their location affects sales."

Lilly watched as Kyle and Jax silently moved into the open space behind Tobi. Jax gave Lilly a quick nod, but Kyle's thunderous expression never wavered, his focus on his speed-demon wife. Lilly wondered if she could distract him, but the thought no sooner moved through her mind than his gaze shot toward her. The glare was brief but fierce enough to let her know he wouldn't tolerate any interference. Unfortunately, Tabby's tequila-fueled courage hadn't gotten the memo to stay quiet.

"Kyle's going to have a stroke if he isn't careful. I'll bet his blood pressure is hovering somewhere close to thermonuclear." Tobi nudged Charlotte and giggled.

"I noticed that. Seems a little over-dramatic for speeding. Even Governor Whistle Cheeks doesn't get bent out of shape about speeding, and God knows I've given him plenty of opportunities." Charlotte's need for speed was well known in law enforcement circles. The last Lilly knew officers tried to avoid her usual routes, hoping to stay off the Governor's radar. What they didn't realize was how critical he was of his wife's driving. He told her years earlier he wouldn't use his position to fix her tickets.

"Ladies, we're going to steal our wives away from you. My mom will make note of any questions or suggestions you might have and pass them along."

Lilly resisted the urge to smile. Kyle might think he was immune to Tabby and Charlotte's attempt to distract him, but she could already see the tension draining from his shoulders. As he and Jax led their wives past her, Lilly wrapped her hand around Kyle's forearm.

"Remember the *post-mission rule*." Lilly watched as Kyle's eyes softened fractionally before he gave her a curt nod. When they'd first become Navy SEALs, her sons' team leader encouraged them to postpone important decisions after missions. He'd emphasized the dangers associated with adrenaline-fueled emotions and asked those he mentored to draw clear lines between their professional and personal lives.

Lilly smiled when Jax McDonald winked at Tobi.

"Sweet cheeks, you are in a lot of trouble. If it's any comfort, you're not alone." Jax's dark hair and blue eyes were so striking, it amazed Lilly that his height was what people remembered. Standing just one-inch shy of seven feet, he was imposing, but she'd always seen the gentle spirit within. Jax gave his wife's ass a firm swat, lifting her up onto her toes. "As for you, Baby, Micah and I plan to explain in detail why it's unnecessary to keep up when your friend thinks she is Max Verstappen."

When the door closed behind them, Lilly turned to find her friends grinning like Cheshire Cats. "I'll bet Gracie doesn't have any clue who Max Verstappen is." Charlotte was vibrating with energy as she gave Tabby a high five and added, "But we do. Hell, we've got our very own fan club."

"I have to admit, I'm surprised Jax would use him as an example because he's hot as hell. Granted, I'm *almost* old enough to be his mother, but that doesn't mean I'm blind." Tabby fanned herself with the sales flyer in her hand.

"Okay, I'll bite. Who is he? I assume he's a race car driver of some sort." Lilly's limited attention span wasn't well suited to sitting for long periods of time, watching cars drive in endless laps around a track.

"Belgian Formula One driver."

Lilly smiled to herself at Charlotte's succinct response.

"He is only twenty-five years old and ranked number one. His list of wins and podium appearances is damned impressive. The man is the very definition of fearless when he's behind a steering wheel." Tabby paused, tapping a perfectly manicured fingernail against her chin, lost in thought for a few seconds, before adding, "I'll bet Tobi knows who he is. I noticed she didn't look confused by the name drop."

"Knowing Jax and his family's connections, he's probably on a first-name basis with half the drivers on the circuit." Lilly snickered when her friends' eyes widened. Throwing her hands into the air in surrender, Lilly laughed, "Okay, okay, I'll ask. I have to admit, it would be great research for a book." The more she thought about writing, the more excited she was becoming. Lilly was so lost in her own thoughts, she didn't realize Tabby was on the phone until her friend told the caller she was on her way.

"Tabby, you can't drive. Good heavens, none of us would be safe behind the wheel. What's happened to send you off this early?"

Before Tabby finished repeating her elderly aunt's story, Tank stepped into the room.

"Ladies, I'll be driving you into town. I'm parked by the rear service entrance. I've already loaded your purses and bottles of water." When they all stared open-mouthed at the club's enormous gatekeeper, he shook his head and smiled. "Come on. You don't want Miss Emily dismantling your favorite boutique, do you? And if they call the police, she'll do something outrageous and end up in jail."

"Oh, shit, he's right. Let's go." Tabby sprinted through the small shop, stopping so abruptly, Charlotte wasn't able to slow enough to prevent their collision. The two of them collided with the door with enough force to rattle the windows. Lilly might not know what was going on, but she wasn't about to be left behind. She'd just hit her stride when Tank grabbed the back of her shirt, lifting her off the ground to keep her from joining the pileup at the door.

Tank shook his head and grumbled something about not being paid enough to chauffer three drunk women to pick up a ninety-five-year-old who was kicking up a fuss in some frou-frou store downtown. Lilly giggled about Tank's disgruntled muttering as he helped the women into the back of one of the oversized black SUVs from the Prairie Winds' fleet. Tank moved around the vehicle to the driver's side and didn't waste any time getting on the road.

"Okay, tell me what your aunt has gotten up to now." Lilly found Tabby's Aunt Emily's stories enormously entertaining. She was also grateful the feisty ninety-year-old was Tabby's responsibility. Lilly wanted to be the old lady who drove her family to distraction rather than the person expected to rein in their wild relative.

"She used the wrong pronouns when speaking to one of the salesclerks. When she was told to use *they/them*, she informed them she couldn't use a plural pronoun to describe one person. As you know, my aunt was an English professor in the days when women weren't supposed to hold such prestigious positions. Well, after a short but very loud discussion, she called me because they were threatening to call the police and the press. She insists they are simply confused about singular and plural pronouns and wants me to help her explain proper sentence structure to them. Can you imagine? This has disaster written all over it."

Lilly agreed. The situation could easily become a political nightmare for everyone involved. She wished Dean and Del had joined them. Her husbands always seemed to find the right words to soothe ruffled feathers.

Chapter Two

Tobi

"THIS IS UNNECESSARY. I don't appreciate being frog-marched across the compound to your office. It's insulting." Tobi was working up a good head of steam as she walked down the corridor toward their private domain. Her heels tapped a steady beat against the wooden floors, each step echoing off the walls and adding to her frustration. "I don't know what you're all pissy about. You tricked me into helping you, and now you're all up in my business about the way I drove the truck."

Stepping through the doorway into Kent and Kyle's office, she wasn't surprised to see Kent standing by the fireplace. His hair was still wet from his shower, making her wonder what had happened during the rescue. He was quick to wash away anything unpleasant after a mission. Kent told her once that he wanted to keep her as far from the violence as possible. She'd appreciated the thought at the time, but as the years went by, she'd started to wonder if the two of them didn't think she could handle the truth about the dangers they faced as a part of their lives outside Austin.

Tobi had learned far more about their missions than they knew. She'd made it a priority early in their marriage to find out as much as she could about what they did as contract agents for the United States military. It had taken her months to get enough details and bits of information to feel like she finally understood the dangers they faced. Tobi never told them what she'd learned, but she was tired of pretending to be clueless.

"You think you are protecting me by keeping me in the dark, but I'm not a fragile china doll, and I know more about your missions than you think I do. If one of the women on your team drives fast, you don't go all he-man on her. I'd wager you all congratulate her on a job well done, and the story becomes another chapter in the team legend. But if it's me... boy, howdy, all hell breaks loose, and I get yanked out of a meeting with club members, tugged along like a naughty toddler to your office so you can punish me for doing exactly what I was told to do. Did you or did you not say, 'Get home as fast as you can, don't get distracted by something shiny on the side of the road.'"

She'd quoted Kent verbatim, and Tobi knew he remembered as she watched his eyes narrow and darken. Everyone assumed Kent was easier to get along with than his twin, but that wasn't usually true. Kyle was more vocal in his protests, but Kent was the one whose emotions ran deep and often deathly silent. She'd learned early in their marriage that Kent West often stood in the shadows, making certain he had all the facts before making a decision and speaking up. Once he'd made a decision, nothing could sway him.

"Members of our team are skilled drivers. They've been trained by the best, and we trust them implicitly."

Tobi was stunned for a few seconds, unable to believe he had the audacity to utter such a blatant insult.

"But you don't trust me? Do you even hear how offensive that is? Fudgesicles, I'm so mad I could just spit." With her hands on her generous hips, Tobi stomped her foot and glared at Kent as he struggled to hide his amusement. "Did you forget about all the defensive driving classes you made me take? I trained with your recruits in self-defense and evasive driving, so your excuse about training falls on deaf ears. You take the blasted cake. I swear to Pete and Re-Pete, you are annoying."

"It's different with you, Kitten." Tobi spun around so quickly that she lost her balance and had to grab onto the back of a chair to keep from toppling over. She hadn't heard Kyle move so close behind her. The damned man moved like a cat, so it was no wonder he'd been able to sneak up on her.

"Why? What's different? The fact I'm not one of your beloved team members? And don't get all snarly with me, Kyle West. I know that expression. You're a split second away from going all big, bad Dom on me, and that isn't going to settle this. Whatever punishment you planned is off the table. Not everything can be resolved naked."

Kyle's only reaction was his arched brow and the ghost of a smile she saw teasing the corners of his lips. He didn't move or speak, but she refused to be intimidated by his silence. Long, torturous seconds passed before he finally nodded once, acknowledging she'd made her point. Tobi tried to hide her relief but knew the two of them too well. There was no way they would miss the way her shoulders relaxed or the silent release of a breath she hadn't known she'd been holding.

This was a discussion that had been a long time coming. Over time, their D/s lifestyle expanded from playing at the club and occasional scenes at home to them dominating almost every aspect of her life. She'd enjoyed a lot of freedom when she and Gracie traveled, but everything started to shift when their business model changed, becoming exclusively remote. Once their twins moved into their boarding school, her husbands closed ranks around her. She noticed the change immediately, and their constant attention quickly became a problem. Tobi felt smothered and became restless.

"Do you think we haven't noticed how unhappy you've become?" Kyle's gaze moved over her in a slow caress Tobi swore she felt all the way to the depths of her soul.

"She's been wound tight for months but didn't bother to confide in us about the problem. What was the word you used earlier? Oh, yeah... *insulting*." Kent stepped smoothly around her to stand beside Kyle. Their mirroring poses were meant to be intimidating, but all she saw was two times the hotness. The two of them always had this effect on her. It started when she met Kyle on the highway during a Texas downpour. She'd given up trying to flag down help from the side of the road and moved to the center of the blacktopped road. Kyle had almost hit her as he battled to see through the pounding rain.

He'd been angry, but she'd instinctively known he wouldn't hurt her. As he'd stomped toward her, Tobi's focus moved from relief someone had finally stopped to a surge of lust so intense, she'd been thrown off her game for several seconds. Kyle's shirt had been soaked and plastered over his broad shoulders, highlighting the six-pack of his abdomen. One look, and she'd felt heat coursing through her body like slow-moving hot lava—desire scorching everything in its path. Her reaction to Kent was the same.

After all these years, looking at them still made her heart skip a beat. Tobi knew from unfortunate experience it was important to remain mindful of her breathing. If she didn't make an effort to pull in each breath, she unconsciously held her breath. She'd made the mistake of sucking in a breath and forgetting to take another more than once. Damn, she hated it when those blasted black dots danced in her vision.

Standing shoulder to shoulder, arms crossed over their chests with their feet shoulder-width apart, Kent and Kyle were mirror images of one another. Tobi fought to remain in place. The heat filling her core was intense to the point, she started to wonder if people could spontaneously combust from lust alone. Damn it all to dead-beat daffodils, she almost forgot she was angry.

"Don't try to flip this around on me. As soon as the kids moved to school, you dropped a net over me, and you've been tightening the strings ever since. Why?" If she hadn't been paying close attention, Tobi would have missed the subtle shift in Kent's posture and the flicker in Kyle's eyes that always meant he was hiding something. Tobi's mind spun with possibilities as she thought back over what she knew about their most recent missions.

"I can practically hear your mind spinning, Kitten." Kyle turned to Kent in time to see his brother grimace.

"Don't look at me. You might as well tell her. She's going to find out sooner or later." Kent didn't volunteer the information, pushing the responsibility onto Kyle. When Kyle didn't immediately respond, Kent rolled his eyes and took her hand in his. Walking her to the sitting area, he settled her on the stone table in front of an oversized sofa. He and Kyle sat on the supple leather Chesterfield they'd recently purchased. She could see Kyle becoming more agitated as the silence stretched between the three of them, but she wasn't going to let him off the hook by starting the conversation. If he'd been holding back important information from her, she wanted to know why.

"As you know, we've been extremely busy with missions to Central and South America over the past few months. We've been working with several agencies that all had valuable but differing intel on an enormous human trafficking ring. Many of the young adults and kids from the United States and Canada that go missing are routed through several hubs in the coastal countries of Central and the northern part of South America."

"There are multiple hubs around the world, but the groups committed to the inter-agency work needed to start somewhere, and these hubs move people from the western hemisphere to the east. Almost all of those missing from the U.S. go south before being sold internationally." Kent's added explanation was educational, but Tobi still didn't understand how any of this affected her.

"I'm going to need more information if you expect me to understand what's going on. I know that you've spent years working to break up human trafficking rings all over the world." When they both stared at her with their mouths gaping open, Tobi shrugged. "I worry, so I've always made an effort to learn as much as I could about your work. You ask a zillion and one questions about what Gracie and I are working on, but anytime I ask you questions, you clam up."

"And naturally, being shut out fueled your curiosity." It didn't escape her attention that Kent's comment was a statement rather than a question, but she nodded anyway. Shifting his attention to Kyle, Kent added, "We should have seen this coming. She's too much like Mom to leave anything alone once she's left out of the loop."

"The dads tried to warn us. We'll never hear the end of

it if they find out they were right." Kent's comment sounded more like a groan than an observation.

It was all Tobi could do to keep from rolling her eyes. Her fathers-in-law had been helping her from the beginning. They would be thrilled to finally be able to rub their sons' noses in their own ignorance. Dean and Del were proud of their duplicity.

"I want to make certain I have this right. You are more worried about facing your dads and having them say *I told you so* than you are about me being frustrated with you for withholding important information from me? Information I can only assume is related to my safety since you have been my blessed shadows for months." She knew her face was turning red the way it always did when she was embarrassed or angry, but, for once, she didn't care. When they didn't respond, Tobi fought the urge to walk away from them until they sorted out their priorities.

"You two are unbelievable, you know that? Boy, oh boy, this frosts my cookies. You could at least tell me why you didn't think I could handle knowing about these missions. And just for the record, if you use that lame excuse of protecting me, I'll go postal."

"Sweetness, protecting you is always our priority. I'll admit we don't always explain things the way we should or in a timely manner, but we always have your best interests at heart."

Kent was using the tone she'd come to associate with PCBS, and if there was anything she hated, it was politically correct bullshit. This wasn't going to be a snow job; it was going to be a full-blown blizzard. Tobi stood up—she'd learned it was better to walk away and let them sort things out than to argue with either of them. They were getting on her last nerve, and she needed some space before she blurted out something she'd regret.

"Kitten, don't go. I know it seems as though we're stalling, and I suppose to some degree, that's true. The real problem is that we know we should have told you about the threats we've received." He paused for several seconds before sighing. "But like every other Dom, we thought we could solve the problem without frightening you."

"Did it ever enter your mind that I'm an adult? I consider myself intelligent enough to participate in decisions that affect me, and I'm fed up with being coddled." Tobi could feel the warning burn behind her eyes and knew her frustration was about to erupt in a flood of tears. Damn it all to hell, crying wouldn't do a darned thing to strengthen the argument she was an adult. Blinking furiously, hoping to push back the tears, Tobi bit the inside of her cheek until she tasted blood. She didn't dare show any weakness if she wanted to make her point.

Wrapping his hand around hers, Kyle pulled her forward, erasing the distance she'd tried to put between them.

"Kitten, our need to protect you is grounded in our love for you and a deep desire to make certain you are happy. We know full well you are capable of handling anything life throws at you—you've proven it time and again."

Tobi knew Kyle was thinking about the abuse she'd endured after her mother died. Her father had taken out his unhappiness on her and taught her brother to do the same.

"This is one of those situations where we made a bad call at the outset, and the damned thing snowballed. Everything that followed compounded our original mistake until we ended up here." Kent's body language and tone were conciliatory, and Tobi felt her resolve weakening. Damn. "The woman we brought back from Panama had been working undercover for two years. She managed to infiltrate the large trafficking ring we've been trying to dismantle. Her cover was blown when she made a phone call. She barely made it out of her apartment before it was raided." There was something about the tone of Kent's voice that made Tobi suck in a breath. She suspected that the phone call was the reason they were so worried about her.

"The cartel Camila worked her way into while in Columbia operates a wide spectrum of criminal activity... drugs, guns, gambling, and human trafficking. There have been several teams working to bring them down, but none of them have been able to make significant inroads until now. Unfortunately, they'd identified the two of us as team leaders." Kyle's tone betrayed his outward appearance of calm. "The phone call Camila made was picked up by their security force. The call was significant because it was a warning. Camila overheard a conversation in the club she managed for the cartel. The men were discussing the best way to distract us. Everyone who knows us knows the answer."

This time, it was Tobi who reached out to grasp their hands. They often smothered her with their need to protect her, but as frustrating as it was, she understood.

"What about Kodi and Kameron? Are they safe? Do we need to bring them home?"

"They are safe. The threat wasn't against them, Kitten." She could hear the certainty in his voice and let out a sigh of relief. Before she could process what he was saying, he added, "The threat was very specific." His pause was too long, and Tobi could feel the tension crackling in the air before he added, "You are the target, Tobi."

"Me? Why me?" Her thoughts were racing so quickly, she was barely able to ask the questions.

"Tobi, everyone knows you are our Achilles' heel."

Kyle's admission brought tears to her eyes, and this time, she didn't have any hope of holding them back. In a well-practiced move, Kyle picked her up and returned to the sofa. Settling her on his lap, she was distantly aware of Kent draping her legs over his own. The position was comforting in its familiarity, and she felt herself melting into them. It had been this way since they'd met. They were her safety net.

"Is this why you didn't want her riding back with me? You could have just told me."

"It is, and yes, we should have told you, but we didn't. Camila was bound and determined to talk to you personally, and we didn't want you to hear this from a stranger." There was a hint of amusement in Kent's voice which piqued her curiosity, but she'd learned years ago that patience was her ally. Pressing her men for answers would be counterproductive.

"I know it seems like we're hedging, but there is a difference between skirting a subject and making certain we don't taint your view. Camila Diaz, the agent Interpol sent to infiltrate the cartel, is a hurricane wrapped in a small package. She has been pretending to be a Domme while running one of the group's favorite kink clubs." Kyle paused, giving Tobi time to process what he'd said, and Kent's grin told her the story wasn't all gloom and doom.

"Kyle's description of Ms. Diaz is lacking. She reminds me a lot of you—a small package of dynamite. Managing the club frequented by members of the cartel would be tough in any country, but it was particularly challenging in Columbia."

Tobi didn't have to ask what Kent meant. She understood how difficult it had been for her and Gracie to build a business in countries where a woman in a leadership role wasn't commonplace. Female leadership wasn't as readily accepted in many nations around the world. Tobi couldn't imagine how difficult it would be in a location where old-school patriarchal society was still the norm.

"Camila is a typical Interpol agent. She doesn't mince words. Hell, she is blunt and brutally honest." Tobi felt Kyle relax beneath her. The small shift was enough to make her follow his example. "She is determined to meet you. We wanted to personally forewarn you. She stormed away from our team as soon as her feet hit the tarmac. The damned woman was looking for you because she'd overheard someone say you were meeting us at the airport. Our people are the best, but their smokescreen won't hold her off forever. She is too much like you and our mom to be held back long."

Tobi felt herself smile. She didn't know Camila, but any woman who could elicit this reaction from her warriors already had Tobi's respect.

"We were aware there were rumors of threats, but we hadn't been able to confirm them. We'd decided to take precautions, but to keep them at a minimum until we could make certain they were credible. We hadn't been able to speak with anyone who had first-hand knowledge until Camila's call." Kent was smoothing his hands up and down the length of her bare legs. The gentle movement was soothing and distracting in equal measure.

"She blew her cover to warn us, so we moved heaven and earth to get her to safety."

"Why didn't Interpol rescue her?" Tobi understood why the Prairie Winds team rushed to Columbia, but she was curious why the agency Camila worked for hadn't stepped up to pull out one of their own operatives.

"Red tape. The same reason we turn down as many agency-assists as we accept. Government agencies are drowning in their own bureaucracy. We're so swamped we're considering putting together another team and opening a satellite location... if we can find one that meets our criteria."

Tobi wasn't surprised by Kent's response. She'd wondered when they were going to realize they were spreading themselves too thin. She and Gracie had faced the same dilemma. She'd always felt as though others had recognized the problem before they'd seen the light.

Kent's hands were heating her skin to a point, her attention was drifting from the subject to her desires. The rat knew the effect he was having on her and smirked before continuing.

"We'll have plenty of time to discuss business later. Right now, we have other priorities." His hand slid up the sensitive skin along the inside of her thigh to tease the dampening folds under her silk panties. Tobi's body responded before her mind registered the shift in their conversation.

"You aren't playing fair." They knew how to distract her. Hell, they'd earned their PhDs in manipulating her body.

"We've never claimed to play fair when it comes to you, Kitten." Kyle turned her face to his, brushing his lips over hers so gently, it reminded her of a soft summer breeze. The fresh scent of the shower gel he favored still lingered, mixing with Kent's fresh scent surrounding her, and it took every bit of her concentration to keep from leaning in to deepen his teasing kiss. His lips were warm, and she could taste the sweet mints he always had in his pocket.

"Tell me about the threats." She felt both men go still the minute she uttered the words. Knowing she was still able to surprise them filled Tobi with pride. Kent and Kyle often joked it took both of them to keep up with her. In many ways, it was true, but the reality of their day-to-day lives was more challenging. Early in their marriage, she'd often felt like they were ganging up on her. She'd had a childhood friend who was an only child. The girl had insisted it wasn't all it was cracked up to be since her parents had already compared notes by the time they talked to her, and there was no one to point the finger at if something went wrong. The situation mirrored Tobi's marriage in many ways.

After the birth of their twins, Kent and Kyle had been too busy to tag team her, and Tobi would be lying if she said she hadn't enjoyed the reprieve. When their children started school, she and Gracie started the Forum Shops. Their business grew faster than they'd ever imagined possible. At the same time, the Prairie Winds team was busy adding operatives to keep up with the number of missions Uncle Sam sent their way. Things started to change when Tobi and Gracie stopped traveling. Kent and Kyle seemed to become obsessed with keeping her close. She'd barely been able to go into Austin without a member of the team tagging along.

"How long have you been hearing these rumors? I assume those from the cartel aren't the only ones you've received." Tobi had no idea why she hadn't seen it sooner. As their trips to Central and South America became more frequent, their preoccupation with keeping her close became more of an issue. She'd wondered why the two of them readily agreed when they were first approached about the twins attending boarding school. They'd run the usual background checks on the staff but hadn't put up any real resistance to the kids moving out from under their roof. "Is this why you didn't go bananas when the kids wanted to go to school in Houston?" Without waiting for an answer, she shook her head, frustrated with herself for not paying closer attention.

"Invitations to attend Hilliard Academy are highly sought after by the best and brightest in the country. We were proud of Kodi and Kameron's achievement, and after their staff cleared our security protocol, we were more than happy to support their decision." Kyle's response sounded rehearsed, and Tobi narrowed her eyes as she shook her head.

"I'll say this for you... that was some of the best PCBS I've heard in a while. I'll bet you had it all worked out, anticipating I'd ask, eventually." She tried to stand, hoping to put distance between them, but they weren't having it. "You probably laughed yourselves silly when I didn't catch on. Boy, I feel like a dope. I probably have one of those cartoon character dunce hats dancing over the top of my head. All I need is one of those wooden stools and a chalkboard to sit next to. Damn, damn, and double flip-flopping damn."

"Be careful, Sweetness. Your language is pushing the boundaries of our patience."

Tobi stared at Kent, knowing her mouth had fallen open. *Fucking hell. Wonder how he'd feel about that response?* She'd probably catch flies if she didn't close her mouth. He had a lot of damned nerve. She'd heard the men and women trash-talking during their workouts. Hell, their banter would make a sailor blush.

27

"You are too educated and beautiful to need vulgarity to communicate."

Good grief, he's really pushing it. Tobi understood any hint of cursing was frowned upon by most Doms, but this time it felt more like a distraction than guidance.

Before she could protest, the calloused tips of Kent's fingers slipped under her panties. Sliding through the slick folds, they found their target with little effort. The sensitive bundle of nerves lit up in response, sending white-hot spears of heat streaking up Tobi's spine. Her head lolled to the side, falling against Kyle's shoulder. She heard herself moan as pleasure steamrolled over her. As hard as she fought to regain control, Kent's determination to steal it was stronger.

"Oh, dear God. How am I supposed to think when you do… *that*. Yes. Right there. Perfect." A release she hadn't seen coming shook Tobi to her core. Brilliant colors burst behind her eyelids, and she heard herself scream. Her entire body felt like it was on fire as wave after wave of molten pleasure streaked through her. By the time her body stopped shuddering with aftershocks, she lay limp in their laps.

Tobi's brain was no longer functioning, and she didn't try to stand because she wasn't sure her legs would hold her. In the back of her mind, she knew their motives were far from noble. Their attention was a well-orchestrated distraction. Damn her traitorous body for short-circuiting her anger. Tobi felt a tide of self-righteous frustration building, but it would be a while before she worked up enough steam for another confrontation. *All those sweet endorphins coursing through my blood make it damned hard to be pissy.*

"Camila is being debriefed by enough alphabet agencies to write a second edition of *War and Peace*, so she's going to be busy for several hours. We missed you, sweetness. Let's go upstairs, and we'll see if we can make you scream our names."

Kent lowered her legs to the floor, and Kyle helped her stand. When she swayed, Kent and Kyle steadied her—their grins of self-satisfaction had her fighting the urge to roll her eyes. Her husbands were incredibly humble, except when it came to Tobi's sexual satisfaction. She often teased them about the correlation between the number of orgasms they gave her and the size of their egos.

Tobi took one step, and her knees folded out from under her. Kyle caught her easily, sliding his arms behind her back and lifting her into his embrace. When they were first married, Kent and Kyle often carried her after a scene—something they hadn't done in a long time. It was humbling to realize how routine and boring their sex lives had become recently. She made a mental note to think of ways to spice things up and sent up a silent prayer her brain would be functioning on enough cylinders tomorrow to remember.

Chapter Three

Camila

"HOW MANY TIMES are you going to ask me the same questions?" Camila fought the urge to roll her eyes at the men and women who'd been sent to debrief her. The only agency on the planet that hadn't sent a representative was the one she worked for. No damned surprise there. Interpol didn't give a rat's ass about her unless she was spoon-feeding her superiors valuable information. Cami had already made the decision to leave the organization she'd been a part of since she was a teen. The only question she hadn't answered was what she planned to do with her time.

Cami was at the top of her game as an operative, but the political climate around the world had changed so much in the past five years, the organization she worked for was barely recognizable. Law enforcement agencies she'd once admired were morphing into weaponized arms of every imaginable political faction with little regard for the laws of their jurisdiction. As a kid being raised by her deeply religious grandmother, Cami rebelled against what she felt were unreasonable limitations imposed on her by the rules and tenets of the church.

After spending her youth resisting what she perceived as the overreach of family, church, and the government's control, it was ironic she was walking away from a career because her peers weren't following the rules. After talking to several members of the Wests' team, Cami discovered she wasn't the only one who struggled with the irony. Sighing to herself, Cami forced her thoughts back to the moment and sighed in frustration. Looking around her, she was amazed the men and women filling the room were still locked in a rapidly deteriorating discussion about who had jurisdiction over the information she'd gathered.

"As soon as I submit my report, my employer will be in touch. As I've mentioned several times, they are responsible for forwarding copies to each of your agencies." Cami tried to keep her voice as even as possible despite her growing annoyance.

"Most of the women funneled through the cartel's bar where you worked were kidnapped on American soil, so we should have full access to the entire report."

Cami couldn't remember the lead agent's first name, but his last name was easy since his nose looked like a beak.

"Agent Hawk, you know Agent Diaz hasn't submitted her report to her supervisor yet. Hell, we've only been stateside for a few hours." Sam McCall's posture shifted slightly; leaning closer to the FBI's lead interrogator had the desired effect. Some of the starch drained from the man's spine as he pushed himself against the back of his chair.

Kent and Kyle disappeared minutes after they'd landed. Every member of the team told Cami their leaders' excuse about dealing with their wild wife's driving was bogus. She'd learned Kent and Kyle rarely went on a mission together. Ordinarily, the team leaders made certain one of them remained behind.

Cami was told the practice harked back to the Old

West when families had more than one husband. One husband stayed behind while the other ventured out for food and supplies. It ensured the wives were safe and meant they weren't widowed in the wilderness. The husband who remained behind was responsible for protecting their wife and children. When she'd first heard about Kent and Kyle West, they'd been described as a throwback to the time when polyamorous relationships were centered around necessity rather than pleasure. Men outnumbered women during the westward expansion, so sharing wives made sense. The safety and security for the family was the reason the practice survived.

Cami leaned back in her chair while Sam McCall explained for the umpteenth time why Camila would submit her report to her supervisor before speaking with domestic agencies. It was the first time any of them hinted she worked for an international organization. When the FBI field agent blinked in surprise, it took every ounce of Cami's willpower to keep from laughing out loud. The man was either woefully uninformed or the world's worst actor.

"Why were we called for this meeting if she isn't going to share any of the information she's gathered?"

"You weren't called to a meeting." Sam's voice had gone from accommodating to frustrated. It was obvious he was tired of the field agent's whining. "As a professional courtesy, you were informed we were returning with an additional American citizen aboard. We have always kept your agency apprised whenever possible. Keep in mind this is a policy we can easily change. I'll be happy to pass along your frustration to Kent and Kyle. It makes our lives easier if your superiors in D.C. prefer being left out of the loop."

Cami saw the flush of anger drain from the man's face.

The agent was a heart attack waiting to happen if he didn't learn to cope with challenges. She had no idea how he'd become an agent, much less the head of an area office. Everything else aside, the man wasn't bad looking, but he didn't hold a candle to the hottie standing in the shadows on the other side of the room.

During the long flight back to the U.S., Cami eavesdropped on Max Dillon and Sam McCall's conversation. She'd learned the former Air Force major had joined the Prairie Winds team two months earlier. It was obvious the Wests had been trying to recruit him before he finally called it quits. She hadn't heard all the details, but it sounded as though there was a family issue that made him want to settle in Texas. Cami's mind was drifting to all the possibilities when her phone vibrated against her palm. Opening the message, she was shocked to see a message from Max.

You really should be paying attention. Sam is reading those jokers the riot act for trying to bully you.

Surely, he knew she wasn't intimidated by the agent heading up the local FBI office. Her position at Interpol meant she outranked him by several rungs on the diplomatic ladder. One word from her supervisor and the man would be out of a job tonight.

I'm dead on my feet, and if Agent Important doesn't can it, I might well start snoring.

His face was in the shadows, but she swore she saw him smile. Damn, the man was a triple threat—smart, driven, and hot. The last thing she needed was a man complicating her life. It would be months before she could adequately assess how serious the threat was to her safety. Members of the cartel didn't take betrayal lightly. They would be looking for their pound of flesh. Then again, if she was sitting at the top of some hit list, why not enjoy the time she had left?

Cami needed to make certain Tobi West understood how real the threats to her life were, and the only way to do so was to spend time with the woman everyone described as a force of nature. It had been easy to find information on Kent and Kyle's wife. She was something of a local celebrity. Not only was she married to two men, but she was the beloved daughter-in-law of Lilly West. Both women kept the local gossip columnists well-supplied with tales of their outlandish behavior, as well as their never-ending philanthropic projects.

"If you don't stop asking the same questions time and again, Camila isn't the only one who is going to be dozing off." The sharp tone in Sam McCall's voice pulled Cami back to the moment. "Max, would you mind showing Cami to the cabin nearest yours? You won't need any supplies, Sage and Jen made sure the place was well stocked." Sam shook his head in disgust, "She looks like she is ready to drop, and I don't blame her. Swear to all things holy this debriefing should have ended an hour ago." Turning to Cami, Sam's demeanor and voice softened.

"Micah will bring you a laptop in an hour or so. He said he was waiting for Gracie's mom to finish the food she was making for the team. Gracie will claim she cooked, but she counts putting meals in a picnic basket as cooking." Waving his hand as if the move would help him stay on topic, Jax shrugged. "Anyway, she wants to deliver your dinner and welcome you to Prairie Winds. Don't let her fool you, she may be bringing you some of the best Mexican food you've ever eaten, but she is going to lord it over Tobi that she met you first. Damn, those two are as competitive as sisters and thick as thieves when one of them is in trouble."

Cami couldn't hold back her laughter. Sam shook his head and smiled.

"Word to the wise—the women at Prairie Winds are amazing, but they are also wild as a Texas storm. They'll be your best friends, keep your secrets, and land you in a peck of trouble before you can blink." Looking around her, Cami noticed every member of the team was nodding their agreement and smiling.

"Thanks for the heads-up. I'll enjoy meeting your wife and look forward to talking to Mrs. West at her earliest convenience. I appreciate everything you've done. Your team pulled me out of a very dangerous situation. After I speak with my superiors, I'll set up a meeting with Kent and Kyle, along with their leadership group. They'll know the local landscape and can help decide what information to share." Cami saw several of Austin's law enforcement elite cringe, and she wondered if the FBI agent's head was going to spin on his shoulders, but she didn't let it stop her from walking out the door.

"I don't think I've ever seen anyone calmly toss a match onto a kerosene-soaked bridge, then walk across it with total disregard for the flames."

"Poetic prose from a major? Who would have thought it possible?" The words were pure sarcasm, but Cami knew he wouldn't miss the note of appreciation in her observation. She felt the warmth of his palm as it settled on her lower back—a gentle reassurance as they made their way across the cobblestone courtyard. He used the subtle pressure of his hand to guide her toward a tiny bungalow on the other side of a group of shops. Max laughed as he explained the purpose of the Forum Shops.

"Tobi and Gracie will be happy to show you around

before things open up this weekend. The main room at the club has been closed for renovations, but I hear the contractors wrapped up everything while we were gone."

Cami felt her breath hitch when he turned her to face him.

"You're going to be Tobi's hero for getting Kent and Kyle out of the country. She was pulling her hair out with their meddling in the project she had headed up for weeks. When the reno was nearly complete, they decided to get involved."

"As in making last-minute changes their wife didn't appreciate?"

"Exactly. I've known Kent and Kyle for years, and it's been interesting to watch a petite blonde package of fury set them back on their heels."

Cami was surprised to hear Max's soft laughter. His had been the first face she'd seen when they pulled her out of her neighbor's sweltering attic. Seconds before thugs broke into her house, Cami slipped out a window with her *go bag* and purse. She knew the elderly man living next door was watching out his window when his backdoor snicked open. Slipping inside, she'd followed his directions without question. The attic was hot but set up as a safe room.

"Did you wonder why your neighbor had a safe room?"

"Is mind-reading one of your many skills, Major?" She let him lead her into the cottage and sighed in relief when cool air wrapped around her. Letting out a breath she didn't realize she was holding, Cami closed her eyes and whispered, "Whoever cranked the air conditioning down to *artic* is a saint." She'd smelled awful by the time the team pulled her out of the small door above an antique wardrobe, and things hadn't improved during the ride to the airstrip. It wasn't until they switched to the Wests' private jet in Panama that she was able to shower. Cami was convinced they'd only allowed her out of their sight because the people sitting nearby were turning a nasty shade of green.

"Please tell me the bathroom has a soaking tub. I'm going to sit in it until I turn into a prune. It's the only way I'll ever feel clean again."

"There is a hot tub behind my cabin—" Before he could finish, Cami interrupted.

"I don't have a swimsuit." Max didn't respond, but his raised eyebrow was all the answer she needed. "Let me guess, no one at Prairie Winds wears anything in the hot tubs."

"I suppose it's possible, but it doesn't seem likely."

She wasn't surprised by his response—after all, Prairie Winds was one of the most prestigious kink clubs in the country. Cami looked around the small cabin and grinned.

"This is lovely. I wasn't expecting anything this nice when they told me I'd be staying in a cabin." Whoever designed the small space understood the challenge.

"I'll point out the safety features, then let you settle in. When you're ready for the hot tub, just knock on my door. My cabin is the one directly behind this one. The hot tub faces the river, which usually proves to be quite entertaining on the weekends."

Cami wondered if Max's observation was sincere or teasing but decided to wait to see if the man had a sense of humor. During the trip back to the U.S., Max seemed content to blend into the background. His conversation with Sam had been the only significant interaction she'd observed. What she had noticed was the way he always appeared to be watching her, but his attention didn't feel creepy. Rather she'd felt as if he was gathering information before making a decision only he was privy to.

Following him to the bedroom, Cami questioned Max's definition of a safety feature when he shackled her wrist with his large hand. She automatically pulled back, but he didn't relinquish his grip.

"Hold still. We need to enter your biometrics into the security system." Max pressed Cami's palm against a panel hidden in a small spot on the wall, and she gasped as it warmed to a point just shy of painful. Before she could comment, the panel cooled, the icy feeling equally uncomfortable. "This makes certain the door will open no matter your body temperature. The reader focuses on a range of spaces between the channels of your prints, calculating an allowance for temperature. It will also send adrenaline levels and other physical factors associated with emotions to the control center."

The door slid open silently, but she hesitated to step into the pitch-black space. Cami's mind locked out everything but the darkness in front of her as mind-numbing fear hit her like a tsunami. She couldn't move, and Cami knew her heart was beating faster with each passing second. Strong arms pulled her back against a muscular chest, surrounding her in warmth as Max spoke. His warm breath moved over the sensitive shell of her ear, eliciting a shudder that moved from her core to the surface of her sensitized skin.

"Step forward. The movement will illuminate the stairs in front of you. Darkness ensures anyone following you into the room won't see the light as the door closes. As you know, every second head start is an advantage."

When she remained in place, Max lifted her off the

ground enough to take a step forward. Blue lights started out as little more than twinkling stars, then slowly grew brighter until she could see a clear path descending steep steps.

"We need to work on your fear of the dark, Camila." It was the first time he'd called her by name. She'd always preferred the shortened version, but the way her full name rolled off his tongue was oddly intimate.

He loosened his hold just enough for her to slide down his firm chest and the sharp curves of his six-pack. Her imagination launched into overdrive as she wondered what he looked like naked. Their bodies remained pressed against one another as her feet finally touched the ground. Taking a deep breath, Cami started to take a step forward, but the movement was interrupted when he was slow to release her.

"Let your eyes adjust before you attempt the stairs." Max's warm breath ruffled the hair at the top of her head, making her keenly aware of the difference in their sizes. The man towered over her, and for the first time, she wanted to let someone else take the lead. After spending almost two years pretending to be a Domme, Cami wondered if she'd ever feel genuine and whole again.

Max's gentle push forward yanked her back to the moment. She mentally chastised herself for becoming distracted. In her line of work, a moment's lapse was often the difference between life and death. She needed to focus. Cami reminded herself just because her mission ended early, the premature exit didn't mean she didn't have plenty of work to do. As soon as she had a laptop, Cami would wrap up the report she started before her home was invaded by cartel enforcers.

Camila sent up a silent prayer of gratitude that she'd

taken time to install perimeter alarms in the small bungalow she'd rented in Columbia. She didn't doubt those silent alerts saved her life—they also gave her time to grab the emergency bag she kept packed as well as her purse. Being anal-retentive about backing up her work on a removable drive paid off. She'd left behind a laptop with nothing on it except fake letters sent to imaginary family and friends.

Pulling herself out of the memory, Cami was surprised to find an open space at the bottom of the stairs. The lights in the small room slowly brightened until she could clearly see three doors with security pads like the one upstairs.

"The middle door leads to my cabin. Press your palm against the pad." She smiled when the door slid open, disappearing into what appeared to be a rock wall. "I've been told the Wests' investment above ground has been eclipsed by their attention to security below ground."

"How long did it take them to complete this project?" Cami was busy taking in her surroundings but managed to ask the question despite her distraction as they walked single file down a dimly lit corridor.

"I'm not sure it will ever be complete. It's ongoing. I do know they are thinking of expanding to another location." Cami could hear a note of interest in Max's voice and wondered if he was planning to head up the satellite location.

"Are you planning to move to the new location?" When he didn't respond, she laughed. "It would explain why you left the military. Most Majors are in it for the long haul, so I'm interested in why you defied the norm."

"I've been asked to head up another Prairie Winds team, but that isn't public information." She stepped aside when they reached another door, but he shook his head. "I asked Micah to clear you for both cabins. I will feel better if you have access to my place in case someone manages to get past the multiple layers of security outside."

She could hear the amusement in his voice and was tempted to turn around to see his expression. Cami wondered what it took to make him laugh out loud. Smiling to herself, Cami couldn't help wondering if he had a sense of humor. *It would be my bloody luck to be attracted to a hot guy who gives stern a new face.*

They entered the second cabin, and Cami was pleasantly surprised to see the small touches he'd added to make the space feel more like a home.

"I can practically hear the wheels in your head spinning, Camila. If you have something to say—say it."

"I was just surprised. You've made the space your own in ways I hadn't expected." She'd never taken time to personalize any of her temporary homes. In her line of work, it was dangerous to give away too much information.

"I understand. People in our line of work don't usually take the time to make a place feel like home because we're not usually in one place long enough. My parents were both in the military. We moved so often, I never completed a school year without moving at least once. I learned at an early age to make the best of any home, no matter how short the stay." He gave a negligent shrug as his finger traced along the bottom edge of a family picture. "It doesn't take much to make a place feel like it belongs to you."

"Is this your family?" She leaned forward to get a closer look at the framed snapshot that seemed to have captured his attention.

"Yes. It's the last picture of us together. I'm sure my cap and gown give away the occasion. I left for Air Force basic two days after this was taken. Three weeks later, my entire family was killed in a car accident." Max took a deep breath, and Cami wished she hadn't asked. She didn't want to bring up painful memories, even though it had obviously been a long time ago. "My brother had just turned sixteen. He was driving when their car hydroplaned during a rainstorm, sending them into the path of a semi."

She looked on as he pulled in a deep breath before turning away from the picture.

"I keep the picture out to remind me how fleeting life can be. Losing the most important people in my life taught me to embrace the moment. Accepting how quickly things can change reminds me to take chances because your whole life can shift between one heartbeat and the next."

Cami appreciated the glimpse Max had given her of the man beneath the stoic exterior. She understood the pain that accompanies loss. Cami barely remembered her mother, and her father spent years in prison for her murder before being stabbed through the heart during a riot.

"The hot tub is on the back deck. I'll uncover it and set out towels while you eat. Don't be surprised if Micah conveniently forgets your internet access codes when he delivers your laptop. He will be convinced you need to rest before submitting your report." When she frowned, Max shook his head. "Prairie Winds doesn't operate like a government agency where everything is predicated on the theory *hurry up and wait*. They believe it's important to take care of yourself and your teammates. Everyone performs better when they are well fed and rested."

She didn't argue the point but knew it was going to be difficult to unwind after spending years working seven days a week. Cami couldn't remember the last time she had a day off. She might not know what her future would look like, but she'd already decided it wouldn't be a repeat of her past. This time, she would take more time for herself.

"Come on. I'll walk you back to your cabin." When she turned to the door leading to the tunnel, Max shook his head. "We used the tunnel to make sure your biometrics were entered and activated." It was important Camila was a part of the set-up rather than simply submitting a palm print. "The tunnel system is reserved for emergencies. The minute you activate the door, everything you do or say is relayed to every member of the team. After this, people will come out of the woodwork if you touch the panel."

Cami was surprised to find her cabin was much closer to his than she thought. The distance seemed further when she was walking through the tunnel. She pressed her palm to the pad beside the back door and smiled when she heard the lock snick open. Prairie Winds' technology was impressive. She'd seen top-of-the-line cameras in the main building and outside as Max walked her to the bungalow assigned to her. There wasn't any doubt there were several more layers of security she wasn't seeing. Damn, it would be fun to get a peek inside their control center. There was very little she loved more than gadgets.

During her stay in Columbia, her access to electronics was limited. The only people who could afford technological luxuries were high-ranking military officials or members of the cartel. She was anxious to get her hands on a laptop that was updated enough to run two programs at the same time.

"Okay, got it. Don't use the tunnel to terrorize the neighborhood." He snorted a laugh and shook his head. "I know the whole compound is wired for sight and sound." She'd have to be blind to have missed the cameras. "The Masters of the Prairie Winds Club's reputation for safety is top tier. Also, there is no doubt Kent and Kyle have put together one of the best special operations teams in the world."

"And there are inherent dangers when you hire anyone who has worked in the Special Forces or for international intelligence agencies." He hesitated for a moment, and before he had a chance to continue, the doorbell rang. When she didn't immediately move to the door, he shrugged and nodded toward the cabin's rear entrance. "We'll continue this conversation in the hot tub. I'll see myself out." Cami moved the short distance to the front door and opened it without checking the peephole, earning a glare from the man and a giggle from the pretty Latin woman standing beside him.

"Hello, Camila, I'm Micah Drake, and this is my wife, Gracie."

"The only reason he isn't reading you the riot act is because you already know it was a mistake to open the door without checking to be certain the boogie man wasn't waiting to torture you. He's brilliant and usually a sweet-heart, but he's still a Dom, and you know how anal they are about safety." The woman breezed past her, making a beeline for the kitchen. Looking around as if she'd expected to find someone in the small space, the petite woman looked confused for a few seconds before plunging ahead. "I thought Max was here." Turning to Micah, she frowned. "You told me he was here. All that sophisticated gadgetry, and you're wrong? Good heavens, you're going to give the local weatherman a run for his money. I swear the more technology they use, the less accurate they are."

"Meteorologist, Baby. If I have to keep reminding you to refrain from using gender-specific titles, there will be consequences." His words would have sounded more

44

threatening if his voice and body language weren't screaming sex-on-demand. Micah Drake had the most intriguing eye color Cami had ever seen. The unique shade of ice-crystal blue, accented by sun-bleached blonde hair, made him look more like a career surfer than the head of security for a kink club. Micah Drake looked like he'd be more at home on a beach than managing communication and logistics at the headquarters of a covert special operations team.

"I'm older than I look, Camila, but I appreciate the compliment." Her expression must have shown her shock because Gracie paused before stepping out the back door.

"My husband can hear some people's thoughts. Lucky for me, he appears to be tuned into your frequency, which means he'll have less time to eavesdrop on mine." The door closed behind her, leaving Cami staring at the flat surface, hoping it would somehow explain Gracie's comment.

"Gracie is in trouble. A lot of trouble. Again. It's true I can catch bits and pieces of thoughts occasionally, but it's something everyone can do if they are paying attention. I'm a Dominant, and by nature, we are observant. I've seen your expression enough times to recognize the meaning."

She wasn't sure what to make of Micah. Her first impression had been that he was easy-going, but he'd quickly proved her wrong. There was an intensity beneath the cool veneer of the man he let surface. Cami wondered if Micah understood how beneficial it was to be underestimated.

"Let's not get off on the wrong foot, Camila. I'm not usually difficult. I'm in desperate need of a vacation, and it isn't going to happen anytime soon."

"I suspect your bosses are asking a lot of you since they are considering expanding. Do you have enough staff to support the added personnel?" His eyes widened in surprise, and Cami was pleased to know she'd broken free from the small box he'd placed her in. People usually assumed agents of her caliber cared little for others. Interpol agents were screened for a lot of things, but the interview process obviously allocated any points for compassion. "Micah, just because my most recent assignment required me to work alone doesn't mean I haven't worked with a partner or team."

"I didn't mean to insult you. My experience with Interpol agents hasn't always been positive." Micah was still holding the laptop, and she wondered if he'd changed his mind about leaving it for her to use. Cami didn't know what soured his attitude toward agents from Interpol, and she didn't want to care. She refrained from rolling her eyes in frustration. Cami hated being judged, and his attitude stung more than it should.

Turning her attention to the containers on the kitchen counter, Cami pulled back the foil and sighed as the aroma of home-cooked food surrounded her. Looking at the mounds of pulled pork flanking perfectly seared vegetables made her mouth water. Piling everything on a warm tortilla, Cami didn't take time to grab a plate before digging in. "Oh, dear God. This is so good." She watched Micah reach for a plate, but Cami shook her head. "No need. I'm perfectly happy eating from these containers. It's delicious. Your wife is an angel."

"I agree. I love everything about Gracie, and Jax feels the same. She is the perfect combination of relaxing calm and raging storm."

"And she can cook. Holy crap, this is the best thing I've eaten in years… maybe forever. I'm torn between eating until I can't move and stashing some of it for tomorrow.

This is a life-altering decision." If she wasn't mistaken, Cami noticed a ghost of a smile before he turned to set the laptop on the small dining table. "Do Gracie and Tobi take turns making food for the team when they return?"

Chapter Four

Micah

MICAH SPUN AROUND so quickly that he almost toppled the expensive laptop onto the floor. Cami's question had been innocent enough, but after living with his friends and colleagues for so long, it was easy to forget not everyone understood the group's idiosyncrasies.

"No. Tobi is not allowed in the kitchen without supervision."

Camila laughed before her expression turned pensive. "Are you serious? Not allowed?" She asked the questions between bites of the food she was obviously enjoying. "Why? Did she try to poison someone?"

"No, but she has tried to burn down a few places. Tobi's heart is always in the right place. Always. But she is a hazard in the kitchen." He took a deep breath and tried to relax. It wasn't fair for him to judge Camila based on his experience so many years earlier with another Interpol agent.

Micah met Julie while they were both seniors in college. It hadn't taken him long to figure out she'd set up their first encounter. He learned later that she'd already been recruited by Interpol. She was under the mistaken impression he would introduce her to his parents, who were career military specializing in intelligence. His relationship with Julie hadn't been romantic, but the sting of betrayal by a woman he considered a friend still lingered.

"I hope you'll stop looking at me and seeing someone else, Mr. Drake." She set the food aside and washed her hands before returning her attention to him. Micah didn't miss the wall of ice she'd built between them, and he didn't blame her for being put off. "Let's get to work. I know you are anxious to return to your wife. I'll submit my report and make certain your laptop is returned as soon as I can secure my own equipment." Gone was the warm, welcoming woman who greeted them at the door. She didn't appear angry—rather, he had the impression he'd hurt her, and he doubted she gave many people the opportunity.

"Camila, I'm afraid I've made a terrible first impression. I'd like the chance to explain." She didn't look at him for so long, he wasn't sure she would. When she finally lifted her gaze to meet his, Micah wasn't surprised to see the pain he'd seen earlier was gone. The woman standing in front of him was righteously pissed.

"By all means, Mr. Drake. Tell me why you disliked me before you walked through the door. Enlighten me. Explain why you've been the only member of the Prairie Winds team who has been aloof, bordering on rude. I'd like nothing more than to listen to your justification before you do me the great honor of showing me how to use a laptop that's at least two years old. Maybe you'd like to explain why you thought it was okay to look down your nose at me when you know nothing about me aside from the carefully crafted background information and professional profile Interpol graciously provided." Her meaning was crystal clear—what he'd read about her was exactly what her agency wanted him to know. It shamed him to think he

49

was shallow enough to pass judgment without seeing for himself.

So much for being an observant Dom.

The back door of the cabin closed with more force than needed drawing Cami's and Micah's attention. Gracie and Max stood side-by-side, wearing similar glowering expressions. Micah knew their anger was going to pale in comparison to Kent and Kyle's frustration. The Wests had been trying to recruit Camila for over a year. They understood and admired her desire to wrap up the human trafficking case she'd worked on for so long. Micah should have put his personal misgivings aside, particularly when Camila compromised her safety and scrapped her assignment to make sure another woman was safe.

"What's going on, Micah? What have you done? Camila was fine when I left, and now she's spitting mad like a cat whose tail made its way under a rocking chair." Gracie's accent grew more pronounced with each word. The small tell was one of his wife's many charms. At this stage, he still had time to salvage the situation. Once she lapsed into Spanish, he'd have no choice but to ride out the storm.

"I'm interested in hearing your answer, as well, Micah." Max's comment didn't surprise him. Max's interest in Camila was no secret. Micah had been in the control room when the team landed at Prairie Winds. Watching the monitors as the operatives exited the helicopter, he'd noted Max's body language as he waited for Camila to step out into the warm Texas sunshine. The newest member of the team stayed close to the woman they'd pulled from a blazing hot attic while the owner of the house was languishing at a cartel-owned nightclub. Kyle West had gone to great lengths to make certain Camila's neighbor had a rock-solid alibi in case anyone spotted them during the quick in and out.

Micah pulled himself back to the moment and sighed. Camila deserved an explanation, and he already knew his reasoning was going to sound lame, but he refused to consider anything less than honesty.

"I was convinced everything about Camila was phony after reading her bio." Turning to her, Micah tried to smile but knew he'd failed when her expression remained cold. "Whoever created your profile didn't do you any favors, Camila. The entire thing is riddled with such obvious disinformation, it's a wonder the cartel didn't make you months ago. They left several openings in the file I was able to follow back to Interpol." Her eyes widened in surprise, and he made a note to show her what he was talking about once the danger to Tobi was neutralized.

"I've known several Interpol agents over the years, and none of them have impressed me. Unfortunately, I didn't give Camila a chance to prove herself above the rest. She has every right to be angry." Micah almost laughed when Gracie started to roll her eyes but paused, looking toward heaven. He wouldn't have called her on the small show of disrespect, but it amused him she censored herself. Gracie was a natural submissive, but she was also fiercely independent. She was as loyal as anyone he'd ever met, evidenced by the fact Gracie still spent a lot of time with her mother and younger brother. His beautiful wife was by far the strongest personality in her family. He and Jax knew that, in many ways, submission was a reprieve for her.

"What is your issue with Interpol agents, Drake?" Max's tone rode the edge between confusion and anger.

"They've been arrogant and dishonest. None of them have been team players, and the one I knew in college went to great lengths to foster our friendship in an effort to connect with my parents. I should have been suspicious when she knew they were members of the intelligence community, but I naively accepted her explanation that the information was common knowledge around campus." He ran his hand through his hair in annoyance. "I didn't know any better because I rarely attended any of the campus social activities."

"You were probably the President of the Nerd Club in college." He glared at Gracie, but she wasn't the least bit repentant.

"Indeed, but it's not actually news." Micah watched Gracie chew on her lower lip—a move that meant she was mulling over how to broach a sensitive topic. She was too considerate to ask what she really wanted to know, so Micah answered the unspoken question.

"Julie wasn't my girlfriend. We were friends—at least, I believed we were. It's not a long story, and I'll explain more later. Over the years, we've had a couple of agents apply for club membership, and none of them have passed the background checks. They've either lied on their applications or misled interviewers about their experience."

"Listen, I get it, and in the end, it doesn't matter. I need to finish up my report and get some rest before meeting Tobi tomorrow."

Micah shook his head. He wasn't going to leave until this was resolved. Pulling out his phone, Micah read a message from Jax.

"I know you think I've given you an older laptop as an insult, but you're wrong. Don't make the same mistake I made and form an opinion based on minimal information."

"I don't remember you being so pretentious, Drake. Let me give you a bit of advice—when you find yourself in a hole, stop digging." Max looked at Micah with barely disguised annoyance before stepping in front of Camila. "You are going to need the hot tub after this cluster fuck. Remember, you don't have to complete your report tonight. As a matter of fact, I'd recommend you familiarize yourself with the equipment, then take a break. I've made the mistake of submitting reports when I was frustrated, and it never ends well."

Camila nodded, but Micah couldn't hear her whispered response. Max smiled.

"I'll leave the front door unlocked. Just walk straight through. I'm going to open a bottle of wine and kick back on the deck. I enjoy watching the old codgers fishing on the river. They are competitive as hell. Most of them have wicked senses of humor and love giving one another hell."

Micah was relieved to see Camila smile again and hoped he could salvage a congenial working relationship after treating her so badly.

"Honestly, Micah, this is so out of character. What on earth were you thinking? You've been hard to get along with for days. You've been out of sorts ever since… oh my God. Is this about what the doctor told me last week?" Micah nodded his head. Hearing the doctor explain how endometrial scarring was causing the intense abdominal pain Gracie was experiencing brought both relief and fear. He'd recommended surgery, and she'd readily agreed.

"Mr. Drake, are you okay?" Camila's question pulled his attention back to the moment, and he nodded. It humbled him to hear her call him Mr. Drake rather than Micah, but he had no one but himself to blame.

"I'm fine, although my lovely wife is right. I've let my fear turn me into an ogre. I owe you both apologies, but I'm afraid they won't be as sincere as they should be until after Gracie is back home, and the surgery is behind us."

Jax kept telling him there was nothing to worry about, but those reassurances were falling on deaf ears. It was embarrassing to realize how overwhelming his life felt at the moment. The entire situation gave him a greater appreciation of Kent and Kyle's concerns about Tobi's safety. If he and Jax had received the same warnings about Gracie, Micah would be out of his mind with worry.

"Cami, I'll make you a deal. You put off judging my husband until after my surgery. It's a simple procedure, but Doms don't deal well with not being able to control everything. And I promise to fill you in tomorrow after your meeting with Tobi. I set everything up because it's a safe bet you'll need to unwind after your chat with my best friend. I love Tobi like a sister, but she is a tough cookie. I'll be waiting by the pool with margaritas and snacks."

Micah stepped forward and extended his hand to Camila.

"I'd like to start over, Camila. I know better than to let my personal life affect my work. I won't make excuses for my atrocious behavior. I took Julie's betrayal personally, and heaven knows, over the years, I've let her take up far too much space in my head." He opened the laptop, pressing the start button. He smiled at Camila when her eyes widened as the screen illuminated, the machine booting up in seconds. "I wasn't kidding when I said this laptop wasn't the relic it seemed." He flashed her a smile he hoped was as sincere as he felt.

"This is what you'll need to use our network." Micah handed Camila a small piece of paper with the codes she'd need to access their network. The access wasn't as broad as their own operatives, but it was secure. "I recommend you use your agency's encryption option as an additional layer of security."

She nodded in understanding before running her hand along the top of the screen.

"Your plan for keeping your equipment safe is actually quite remarkable. I had to leave my laptop in Bogotá, but it was as old as it looked. There wasn't anything on it anyone would find remotely interesting. I kept everything on my portable drive."

"As you know, in our line of work, it's never a good idea to lay all your cards on the table. I make every effort possible to make certain any equipment assigned outside the main building or training center is disguised as older equipment. We rarely lose computers to theft from cars or operatives' homes. Those who have had break-ins had their gaming equipment stolen, but the thieves left their laptops."

Micah was pleased to see Camila was familiar with the operating system. The small drive she inserted flashed quickly on the screen, and he was impressed with its capacity. He made a mental note to ask her about the technology as her fingers flew over the keyboard. Gracie nudged him and tilted her head toward the door. Micah nodded as they slipped from the small cottage. They were finished delivering food, so Micah started the side-by-side and turned back to the compound's large garage.

Jax was waiting for them inside the garage, his expression a mix of curiosity and concern.

Chapter Five

Jax

"HOW DID IT go with Camila?" Jax already knew things hadn't gone smoothly. Micah's response to his question about how much longer they would be wasn't the only heads-up he'd received. Max Dillon was livid. The former major's text had been scathing. Initially, Jax was confused. He'd never known Micah to greet visitors with anything less than warmth. Hearing how he'd treated Camila was baffling.

The Interpol agent scrapped her mission to warn them Tobi was being targeted by the South American cartel she spent months infiltrating. Kent and Kyle had been trying to recruit Camila and didn't waste any time pulling her out of Columbia.

"You already know it was an unmitigated disaster, or you wouldn't ask. Fuck me, I'll probably be looking for a job by tomorrow morning." Jax knew better, and so did Micah, but his comment spoke volumes about his friend's feelings of guilt about his meeting with Camila. Knowing Micah was worried about their wife made the news he had to share all the more troublesome. Micah and Gracie moved to the garage's walk-in door, but Jax stepped forward to block the exit. Micah's eyes widened in surprise, and Jax could see the moment the other man sensed something was wrong.

"The clinic called. Gracie, they asked you to come in so they can redo a blood test." Every bit of color drained from her pretty face, and she stumbled while trying to make her way to a nearby seat. Micah wrapped his arm around her waist, steadying her until she was seated on one of the wooden benches inside the garage's spacious office. Jax and Micah sat on either side of her, each taking one of her trembling hands and wrapping it in their own. "I don't want you worrying too much about this until we have some answers. One of the screens they ran on the sample you submitted was exposed to another sample. The initial screening showed a few questionable biomarkers, but it's possible those are the result of the contamination."

"How could the lab make such a huge mistake? Christ, is this the laboratory at her doctor's office?" Before Jax could respond to Micah's question, Gracie shook her head.

"No. He told me they were sending the test to another lab because his techs were both out. One has a new baby, and the other is ill." She took a deep breath, and Jax could almost see her pulling strength from mid-air. Damn, she was the strongest woman he knew. "Can we go to another lab? I know CeCe specializes in pediatrics, but do you think she would let us use her lab?"

"Already arranged. She's waiting for us at the hospital. Let's go." Jax pulled her to her feet and turned to leave. Before he could take a step, Gracie tugged on his hand to get his attention.

"Thank you." She turned her attention to Micah and tried to smile. "This explains why you've been so antsy. You were tuned into the lab's blunder rather than anxiety about the surgery. As soon as we get this straightened out, you'll be back to your usual cooperative but bossy self."

They made the short trip to CeCe Barnes' medical facility in record time. It wasn't far from Prairie Winds, and Jax drove well above the speed limit. Cameron Barnes, CeCe's husband and a retired CIA agent, stood leaning against one of the pillars at the front entrance. Jax smiled and shook his head as they approached the man who always seemed to be up in everyone's business.

"I'll wait while you take Gracie inside. CeCe is waiting for you at the front desk. I want to talk to you while Gracie is with Cecelia." Jax didn't miss the note of concern in Cam's voice and wondered what had happened. He smiled at Gracie and added, "Please don't worry. CeCe has this covered. She'll take good care of you. When I found out she was coming back to the hospital, I insisted on driving her. I think you'll find she is in full doctor mode and wasn't the least bit happy I knew who'd called to arrange this meeting."

Jax could only imagine how frustrated CeCe was that her husband was blatantly violating the rules of confidentiality she was legally bound to follow. Cam simply didn't care. The man was as sexually dominant as any Jax had ever met, which meant he assumed everything in his submissive's life should be an open book. His status as a *retired* agent was also questionable at best. In Jax's experience, the CIA was more than a little reluctant to let their most experienced agents go. They pulled them back in at every opportunity. It was probably in Cam's best interest to stay busy—Jax suspected it was the only thing keeping his lovely wife from strangling him.

"Hi, Gracie." Dr. Cecelia Barnes made her way across the spacious atrium between her clinic and the hospital she'd built to accommodate her growing practice. Dressed in ripped jeans, a low-cut floral blouse so bright it hurt his eyes, and strappy sandals, CeCe looked more like a college student than a renowned pediatric surgeon. "We're going to do two blood draws. I want to make certain we have enough for the screens I've ordered. As you know, this isn't my area of expertise, but I've consulted with some of the best in the field. We plan to keep you apprised of not only what we're doing but why."

Jax felt Gracie relax beside him and was grateful CeCe hadn't passed his pretty wife along to one of the physicians on the hospital's ever-growing staff. CeCe's gaze moved to Micah before settling on him. She smiled and shook her head.

"Sorry, but you'll have to stay out here. We've had to tighten things up due to an uptick in local flu cases." When Micah started to protest, she shook her head. "I promise we're going to take very good care of her. I'm not leaving her side. We won't have all the answers for a few hours, but we'll have the important ones sooner. Give us an hour or two."

"Can we sit with her while she waits for the results?" Micah's question was met with a frown.

"No, I'm sorry. Once we've screened her for flu symptoms, we won't want her back in a public area until we're convinced we don't need anything else. My staff will keep you updated. I won't come out personally unless there's a problem. My priority is sticking to my friend like glue." It was the first break he'd seen in her professional persona, and Jax was grateful to hear her refer to Gracie as a friend rather than a patient. It was easy to understand why parents from all over the world brought their kids to Dr. Barnes.

Pulling Gracie into his arms, Micah buried his pale face in her hair. Jax couldn't hear what his longtime friend whispered in her ear, but her eyes were glassy with unshed tears when he released her. Jax grasped her shoulders, ignoring everything around them, and focused all of his attention on the most important woman in the world.

"We will be right here waiting. CeCe's staff is top-notch. We are going to get results we know are accurate. We'll deal with whatever arises, Cariño." Jax rarely took advantage of his parents' connections or money, but he wouldn't hesitate to use everything at his disposal for Gracie. He was hesitant to let her out of his sight, but they were all anxious to get these tests behind her. Watching Gracie disappear through the automatic doors made his heart squeeze so tight, it stole his breath for several seconds.

"I've never loved anyone as much as I love Gracie. I'm not sure what is worse, my fear of losing her or seeing the haunted look in her eyes." It was the first time Jax had heard his friend admit how worried he was about Gracie. The change in Micah had been evident from the moment her doctor mentioned surgery. Removing the lesions in her abdomen would alleviate the pain she was experiencing, and the doctor's prognosis had been excellent. He'd assured them the risks were minimal, but no medical procedure was guaranteed safe.

Stepping out into the sunshine, Jax and Micah moved to the marble bench where Cameron Barnes sat scrolling through his phone. Jax smiled when he noticed the photos the proud father was viewing. CeCe was the center of Cam's universe, but his kids were his pride and joy. Slipping the phone back into his pocket, Cam motioned for them to join him.

"I'll get right to it. CeCe assured me these tests don't require a lot of time when they are done right, so I don't want to waste a lot of time." Jax almost laughed out loud. Idle chit-chat was never on Cam's to-do list. As if sensing his amusement, Cam's eyes narrowed before he continued. "The tech who contaminated Gracie's original blood sample is no longer employed. While the mistake was honest, his attempt to cover it up was not. Thanks to Carl's internet handiwork, the man will be lucky to get a job slinging hash."

Jax could only imagine what Cam and CeCe's computer-savvy third had set into motion. Jax knew Cam had been enormously relieved when CeCe readily accepted Carl Phillips into their lives. Their friends enjoyed watching the interaction as Carl's laissez-faire attitude settled Cam in a way nothing else ever had.

"Now, I've been doing a little digging into Camila Diaz's background. I wanted to know if there were any red flags in her personal or work history." Cam pushed his fingers through his dark hair. For a man whose reputation as a ghost in the field, the move was telling. "Nothing. Nada. Zilch. Her record is exemplary. Her background hasn't been scrubbed. There were a few instances when she ignored orders, but she always landed on her feet. I met her years ago and was happy to learn Interpol didn't change her. God only knows they would have tried."

"She was close to confirming the identities of the cartel's leaders. Having those names will be a critical part of shutting them down." Jax was playing devil's advocate, hoping it would push Cam to get to the damned point.

"Cami has the information she needs to identify the principal players. She stayed because she wanted to lock down the details of the trafficking route. Finding all the houses where they held victims awaiting transport was the only piece she hadn't finished. The threats to Tobi were credible, and Cami knew she had to make a choice. She had a few of the locations, and Interpol will try to track the activity via satellite to avoid anyone realizing they're being watched."

Jax hoped the bastards were torched for what they were doing.

"I appreciate the update. Kent and Kyle are meeting with Camila tomorrow morning."

"No matter what she finds out today, Gracie is going to need you both. I'll sit in on the meeting. I know I'm not usually the most optimistic man around, but this time, I think we're dealing with someone who is exactly what she seems."

"Essentially?" Micah voiced the question before Jax could voice the same concern.

"In the cartel's club, Camila was a well-respected Domme. She trained submissives but never had sex with them. She should get a damned Academy Award for her performance. How a natural submissive pulled off this scam for months on end is astonishing." Cam shook his head and chuckled. "She's not a switch. Camila is a sub. Pretending to be someone you're not isn't easy under any circumstance. It's nearly impossible when your life and the lives of so many others depend on your performance being spot on."

Jax wondered where Cam was going with this conversation. The man was infamous for taking the scenic tour on the way to the point. Cam had an agenda—that much was easy to see. The real question was, what was the man's endgame?

"Interesting psychoanalysis, but what's your stake in this, Cam?" Micah must have been as tired of the public relations nonsense as Jax was.

"Christ, Micah. It's no wonder Cami wanted to kick your ass. Don't think for a minute she couldn't. She's a fourth degree black belt and a devoted Krav Maga student. She may be little, but she is fierce."

Jax and Micah both laughed out loud. It was obvious Cam knew more than he was letting on.

"Listen. You said you were going to get to the point. Stop stalling and trying to distract us and spit it out."

Chapter Six

Cam

"I TOLD CECE it wouldn't work. The story isn't interesting enough to drag out very long." Cam leaned back against the concrete wall behind him and sighed. "I trained Camila as part of a cross-agency pilot program. Originally, Camila was a Federal Bureau of Investigation recruit. She is brilliant and aced every written test they put in front of her. Her physical skills were remarkable, but it was her ability to read people that set her apart."

"So, why didn't she stay with the FBI? Bigger fish to fry with Interpol?" Cam looked at Micah, hoping it conveyed enough disdain to shut the man up. No such luck. "Did she fail the final? Fall in love with a teacher?"

"No." Cam should have known better than to give these two a curt one-word answer. All he'd done was throw gas on the fire. "Unknown to anyone, including Camila, members of her extended family had ties to the syndicate. During a surveillance training mission, things went south—fast. I can't share the details, but after that night, it was clear she was better suited for international work." Pausing to gather his thoughts and decide how to best proceed, Cam hoped the two men sitting beside him understood what a valuable asset Camila would be to the Prairie Winds team.

"If Camila Diaz thinks the threats to Tobi and members of the team are credible, you damned well better listen. Her bosses are furious with her for protecting a woman they would easily write off as collateral damage."

"I love Tobi West. She's like another sister to me. I'm grateful Ms. Diaz chose to protect her. I don't like hearing any innocent referred to as collateral damage, but I can't honestly say I'm surprised. The whole world has gone fucking insane."

Cam agreed with Jax. Not a day went by when he didn't worry about his children's future. He'd spent his entire adult life dealing with the seedy side of humanity, and he'd never been as worried about the future as he was now.

"I haven't had an opportunity to speak with Camila other than to promise I'll help any way I can. She is the only one who can tell you why she made the call. What I can tell you is that she's honest to a fault. Ask her—whatever she tells you will be the truth. I've never known her to sugar-coat anything. Her skill set is undeniably impressive, but that's not the only reason the Wests have been recruiting her." Cam wasn't sure Jax or Micah appreciated his insight, but they'd do well to treat the petite agent with the respect she deserved. Before they could respond, the clinic's heavy glass door swung open. Gracie burst through, laughter making her seem as though she was walking on air.

"All the tests came back negative... well, except for that pesky one saying I need more metal in my blood."

"Iron. Geez, Gracie, you're going to give my lab a bad reputation if you keep saying *metal*."

Cam pulled his laughing wife against his side, relishing the way her body felt as it vibrated with amusement. He was relieved CeCe was able to give their friends the good news. Cam hated to admit—even to himself—how worried he'd been about Gracie.

"She is anemic. She needs to stop dieting and rest."

"Thank you, CeCe. I'm sure you understand what a huge relief this is."

Cam couldn't remember the last time he'd seen Micah Drake overcome with emotion. Prairie Winds' Chief of Security was known for his by-the-book approach to the protection of those he considered *in his care*. The same intensity was reflected in his persona as a BDSM Dominant. It didn't take Gracie and her husbands long to say their goodbyes and head home. Cam was hoping to do the same. Getting his beautiful wife and submissive home and naked couldn't happen soon enough.

Twenty minutes later, with CeCe sitting in the passenger seat, Cam drove out of the clinic's underground garage. CeCe hadn't known he'd intervened during the facility's planning process to add the private parking lot. Dr. Cecelia Barnes underestimated the security threats directed at her. Most were mundane. Often the problems were the result of overzealous parents trying desperately to get help for their children. Those were as easily understood as they were efficiently dealt with. He attributed her laissez-faire approach to threats falling at the other end of the spectrum to CeCe's immersion in her work.

Cam considered himself dedicated, but his wife took the term laser-focused to an entirely different level. Carl Phillips, the third in their relationship and a retired Navy SEAL, was equally concerned. Carl was the only other man Cam allowed to touch CeCe. He was also the only man Cam had ever had a physical relationship with, and Carl was only submissive to Cam. Their relationship was unconventional but suited them.

It was difficult to pull off any polyamorous relationship outside the kink community—it would be particularly challenging since theirs was a unique situation. One of the things Cam loved about his fellow kinksters... they were the most accepting people he'd ever met. Cam still owned Dark Desires, the BDSM club he started in Houston, but he rarely played there anymore.

Over the years, Cam learned the high protocol he'd once considered important wasn't the key to connecting with his subs. Earning their respect by providing everything they needed was far more effective. Often those needs were about feeling safe and secure in his care, but more often, it was about pushing their boundaries and helping them grow in ways they'd never considered. Watching CeCe from the corner of his eye, Cam smiled to himself when he noted the way she was wringing her hands in her lap. They were always in tune with one another's moods. Her nervousness would play in perfectly with his plans.

"Carl is waiting for us. I called him while you were finishing up with the lab staff. He was in agreement—you deserve something special, Pet." They were going to reward her. CeCe never hesitated to help someone out, and today hadn't been an exception to her generosity. She'd sacrificed a rare day off to help a friend. Within minutes they were home.

Walking across the large patio, Cam watched CeCe's expression as he directed her to the enclosed patio where Carl was waiting by the pool. When they built the house several years ago, Cam enlisted design help from a Florida pool builder he'd seen on television. Cam wanted the hot tub to be surrounded by a natural stone grotto large enough for a minibar and storage cabinet. Water fell in sheets over the top of the grotto's natural rock roof, giving anyone inside a measure of privacy. Their kids and their group of friends loved the pool's water slide and lazy river, but the intimate feeling of the grotto was his favorite.

The sun had set, and darkness wrapped around them as he and CeCe stepped through the fence's heavy wooden gate. CeCe gasped when she saw the grotto illuminated by the flickering light from dozens of candles. Carl leaned against the rough wall of rock with one knee bent so his right foot was propped on the outside of his left. Carl's pose was casual, but his expression was anything but. The fire in the other man's eyes threatened to burn Cam and CeCe to ashes as they approached.

"Sweetness, you have on too many clothes. Strip. I want you naked. Now." The last word was spoken with enough force to pull her attention away from the romantic scene Carl had created. Now that they were closer, Cam could see fresh flowers set around the interior of the grotto. How the hell the man had managed to get bundles of brightly colored flowers in such a short time was a question for later. For now, Cam was content to enjoy the benefits of Carl's resourcefulness.

Watching the woman who held his heart strip off the soft cotton scrubs she favored was a visual treat Cam knew he would never grow tired of watching. Dr. Cecelia Barnes was always challenging herself to do more... do it better and do it faster. He'd never met anyone more driven than the brilliant woman standing so close, Cam felt the air shift around him when she pulled her top over her head.

"We're going to be here all night if you don't kick it up a notch or two, Pet." Cam knew CeCe hadn't missed the implied threat when she hurried to drop the loose-fitting pants. The delicate lace bra and panties were sheer enough to be little more than temptation personified. Damn, he would never complain about her obsession with sexy lingerie. He'd be eternally grateful for his sister-in-law's shopping addiction. "I see Camille has sent you another care package."

CeCe's sister was married to Adam Weston, Cam's former right-hand man and the current manager of Dark Desires. When they first moved to Austin, Cam traveled back to Houston several times a week in a misguided attempt to continue handling the day-to-day operations of the kink club he'd founded. When it became clear the Agency had no intention of letting him fully retire, Cam finally admitted it was time to prioritize. He'd put the club in Adam's capable hands and focused on helping CeCe build her dreams.

"Camille uses me as an excuse to shop. She believes the money you spend on gifts is exempt from her husband's desperate attempt to rein in her spending." CeCe gave a negligent shrug as she opened the front clasp of her bra and let the pretty scrap of lace slide down her arms.

Cam struggled to contain his laughter. CeCe knew her sister too well, and he didn't doubt his wife's explanation. The two women had been close confidants for as long as he'd known them. He often said they would have grown apart if it hadn't been for text messaging. They rarely had time to engage in long phone conversations but would text intermittently at all hours of the day and night.

"I find it interesting you folded those sexy bits of noth-ing and carefully placed them on the scrubs tossed aside like they are yesterday's news."

Cam chuckled at Carl's observation. As a cryptologist, Carl Phillips' mind caught and cataloged every detail, no matter how insignificant the information might appear. Carl had been telling Cam for several months their submissive was teetering on the edge of burnout, and this was further evidence he was right.

CeCe ignored Carl's comment. Cam glanced at Carl, who gave him a knowing look. CeCe's gaze moved to a nearby table, her eyes widening when she saw frosty glasses.

"Did you get Tobi's margarita recipe? Tobi's recipe is a national treasure. Please tell me one of those is for me." When he and Carl laughed at her nonsense, CeCe's eyes lifted toward heaven. "Thank you." Cam looked at her in question, and she shrugged. "When you told me Carl was waiting for us, I sent up a prayer to my guardian angel asking for something cold and refreshing—preferably with a high alcohol content." Her slender shoulders lifted in a quick shrug as she shook her head. "Testing Gracie was stressful. I love her to pieces, and I was terrified I wouldn't be able to give her the good news she deserves."

It was humbling to realize how invested CeCe had been in her friend's medical scare. She hadn't given any outward sign of anxiety. Being forced to hide her stress when dealing with patients and families had to be draining. It was also a dose of reality to know that once again, Carl was miles ahead of him when it came to CeCe.

"Oh my God, this is so good." Cam shook his head as CeCe gulped down half her drink. "I'm pretty sure my guardian angel is a lush—it's probably why she was assigned to me." Cam shook his head and chuckled. Damn, she was fun. It didn't matter how intense the situation was or how high the stakes were—CeCe always brought everything she had to the table. "I'm convinced I'm her last assignment. It would be cruel for God to expect her to take on someone else after dealing with me."

"Baby, you are in excellent company. The angel in charge of assigning guardians must have had a hell of a drinking problem. You, Tobi, Jen, and Lilly should have been assigned a *team* of guardian angels."

"I'm not sure team is the right word, but flock doesn't sound right either. Gaggle? No, that's geese. Band? No, that's gorillas and musicians. Fever? Drat, that's stingrays. Bet you didn't know that one."

Cam suspected she was mocking them, but he wasn't certain until she burst into laughter.

"Pet, you are skating on a very fine line between amusing and disrespectful." Cam heard the growl in his voice underscoring his words and was pleased to see her reaction. He watched her dramatic, dark eyes widen before dropping in an unspoken apology.

"Don't you love the way she so easily accepts being naked? There is nothing in the world hotter than a confident woman whose intelligence is only surpassed by her compassion."

"A group of butterflies is a kaleidoscope. I always loved that one." Cam and Carl both chuckled as she shrugged. "Sorry, I'm a science nerd. What can I say?"

"Baby, you are a ray of sunshine. Come on, we have plans for you, and they don't include a lesson in the correct labels for animal groups." Carl tucked CeCe's hand into the crook of his arm, leading her into the grotto. Cam was already stripping out of the clothes he'd thrown on in a rush to drive CeCe to the medical facility. He'd dressed in a hurry, but he could reverse the process even faster.

Chapter Seven

Camila

CAMI SMILED TO herself when she received confirmation her detailed report and attached letter had been received by her handler. She'd attached a simple confirmation of her earlier resignation letter because she knew her handler hadn't taken the first letter seriously. It had taken her a year to convince the man she deserved his respect. He'd taken one look at her and fumed she'd been assigned to him as a punishment for a mission that had gone so far south, he'd dreamed about Cape Horn Rock Hopper Penguins for months.

"I heard about those damned penguins for months." Cami rolled her eyes when she realized she'd spoken aloud. *Talking to yourself is a bad sign, Camila.* She could hear her mother's sweet admonishment and laughter echoing in her mind. Shaking her head, hoping to clear the memory of how much had changed in the last couple of years, Camila stood so quickly, she almost sent the small chair over backward.

Good grief, nothing like tearing up your free digs. Maybe the hot tub will help. Naked in a hot tub with a man who made her think about her own pleasure for the first time in two years… *What could go wrong?*

After a quick shower, Cami pulled her long, dark hair

up into a messy bun. The shorts and tank top in her bag would have to be good enough. Luckily she'd stashed a pair of sandals inside the boots as well. Walking the short distance to Max's cabin, she wished she'd taken time to search the small kitchen for some liquid courage. It had been a long time since she'd spent time alone with a man she found attractive.

Cami's head was shouting all the reasons she shouldn't even consider taking this risk, but her feet weren't listening. She raised her hand to knock and froze. Her clenched fist was still suspended in the air when the door opened several seconds later.

"I wouldn't have taken you for a coward, Camila." She heard the challenge in Max's voice but refused to take the bait.

Walking passed him when he stepped aside, Cami tried to ignore the delicious way he smelled. One of the things she'd missed while in South America was the clean scent of American men. Members of the club she'd managed in Columbia subscribed to the more is better school of thought. It seemed a point of pride to see how much cologne they could splash on before leaving the locker room. More than once, Cami had blamed the stench for the fact the paint was always peeling in the men's dressing area.

"Did you send a copy of your report to the Wests?" Cami turned to face Max, raising a brow in question.

"No, why do you ask? I can't imagine it is standard operation procedure in the military to submit reports to civilian organizations." The corners of Max's mouth twitched as he studied her.

"No, we wouldn't have sent them outside our own organization. I didn't mean to insult you or question your professionalism. I'd like the opportunity to read it, if and when it's cleared for release." Max paused to let her mind catch up. It was easy to see fatigue dulling her eyes, and he didn't want to overwhelm her. "Check your email. I forwarded a copy of the report Prairie Winds submitted to Interpol and a dozen other agencies." He motioned for her to proceed him into the small kitchen. "If you'll grab that,"—he motioned to a plate laden with fresh fruit and slices of cheese—"I'll bring the beverages." She grinned when she noticed a large bottle of ginger ale sitting on a tray with two ice-filled glasses.

"You've done your homework. I'm impressed."

"I don't want to give away my source. Letting you believe I'm resourceful seems like a better plan."

Cami smiled as they stepped out onto the small deck. The hot tub sat at the end with the best view of the river. Fairy lights twinkled in the overhead rafters, bathing the bubbling water in their soft glow. The soft strains of classical music swirled around her, and Cami felt herself relaxing, despite the fact she was about to step naked into a hot tub with a man she barely knew. She set the plate on a small table before taking the drink he held out to her.

"Thanks, this is great. I haven't had any ginger ale since before I left for Columbia. The cartel only allows certain products in their area. That's their official line."

"Which translated means the only products sold are those they own a stake in." Max's understanding of the situation was no doubt due to his military experience.

She appreciated not needing to explain the details of life under the cartel's dominance. Nothing could have prepared her for the stark reality of living in a community where one group controlled even the most minute details of everyday life.

Camila stared at Max's throat as he drained his own drink before pouring another.

"As anxious as I am to hear about every aspect of your assignment, I'd like to table that discussion. Let's focus on decompressing tonight. Living under those circumstances for as long as you did requires a tremendous amount of energy. Your assignment would drain even the most hardened heart."

She'd trained for long-term missions and had been warned about the aftermath. Cami had been prepared for every aspect of the mission except the overwhelming sense of loneliness that plagued her the entire time. Her despair was compounded by the role she played. Pretending to be an experienced Domme was exhausting.

"Where did you go, Camila?"

Max's softly spoken question pulled her back to the moment as he pushed a stray lock of her hair back over her ear. When did he move? How had he gotten so close without her noticing his change of position?

"I don't like the spark of fear that flashed in your eyes when you realized how close I'd gotten. It's a hell of a compliment to know you allowed your guard to drop enough to be vulnerable with me." Max used his fingers to grip her chin with enough strength to make certain she understood the implied command to keep her gaze locked on his. "You are safe, Camila. I will never hurt you... unless you ask sweetly." His rakish smile made him look younger, and Cami found herself staring into his brilliant blue eyes, lost in the layers of color she hadn't noticed earlier.

"I was thinking about how unprepared I was for the loneliness of being undercover alone for so long." Pulling her gaze from his, Cami turned her attention to the wisps of steam rising from the bubbling surface of the hot tub. "You start the mission feeling ready because you've trained for so many different scenarios, but the reality of being on your own for such an extended period of time is overwhelming."

Max nodded his understanding but didn't respond other than to take her hand and move to the edge of the hot tub.

"The work you did in Columbia is already paying off. Several of the key players have been detained. The information you gave the Wests, combined with details provided by the men who were pulled in for questioning, has led to the rescue of more than a dozen young women. The oldest victim is seventeen—the youngest is ten."

Cami felt herself sway as she absorbed the enormity of what Max was saying. When she opened her mouth to begin a barrage of questions, Max shook his head. "Not tonight, Camila. Kent and Kyle will gather as much intel as they can during the night and give you an update before your sit-down with Tobi."

Cami took a deep breath and nodded. As anxious as she was to hear what was happening with her case, it would be easier if she was given all the information at one time. Before she could respond, the sound of his soft laughter brought her up short. "I'm convinced you deserve an Emmy. Your mind wanders as easily as any submissive I've ever met." When she stiffened, Max shook his head. "Pretending to be something you aren't is never easy. Hell, undercover work is damned tough when it is short term. Agencies all over the world recognize the inherent dangers of long-term immersion among criminal elements. Playing a role that is counter to your personality and sexuality would be torture for a natural submissive."

Cami's heart understood what he was saying, but her head was having trouble accepting someone she'd only just met managed to peg her so perfectly.

"I love that expression—confusion and surprise. Two looks guaranteed to make any Dom sit up and take notice." He paused long enough for her attention to refocus on him before his body language shifted. "Take off your clothes, Camila. We'll talk more after we are settled. Texas weather is fickle this time of year, and I don't want to risk stalling until a storm pops up."

She understood his concern. The towering cloud bank she'd watched build slowly along the western horizon before sunset hadn't set off the weather alarms on her phone, but that didn't mean the situation couldn't change in a matter of minutes. The last place she wanted to be during a Texas thunderstorm was sitting in a hot tub. Cami wasn't scared of a little rain, but she had an enormous amount of respect for lightning.

"I'm curious, Camila. Do you always have trouble following directions?" Damn. She'd been lost in her own thoughts again. At this rate, Max was going to think she had a couple of screws loose or that she was deliberately ignoring him. She peeled out of her clothes before her mind had time to consider the wisdom of naked water games with the hottest man she'd ever met. After the sun set, the temperature dropped enough. Cami shivered when the breeze moved over her bare flesh. "Fucking hell, you are gorgeous."

Max's comment was unexpected, and Cami felt her face heat as embarrassment washed over her. Despite the deep tan she'd gotten in Columbia, Cami knew her face was flushing deep rose, bordering on something closer to scarlet. She'd played the role of a Domme for two years, training more submissives than she could count. Cami was strict but fair, and subs never left a session with her without getting what they needed. That wasn't to say what they needed and what they wanted was always the same— it wasn't, and it was a lesson she was only too happy to teach them.

Warm hands encircled her waist, and Camila squeaked when her feet left the ground. "What the ever-loving waddling ducks?" It took her several seconds to recenter herself enough to recall where she was and who'd lifted her into a small spa filled with water hot enough to take her breath away. "Shit. Hot. Hot. Hot."

"If you had listened, you could have gotten in slowly. Since you seem to be drifting in and out of touch with what's happening around you, I decided it was more expedient to help. Given the glowing reports we received from your handler, your disconnection is either a sign of your instinctive trust in me or the lingering effects of an adrenaline crash. My ego prefers the first explanation."

Cami wished she could fire off a witty response, but she suddenly found it very hard to focus on anything other than the man standing in front of her. Hell, it was probably a good thing she hadn't been paying attention when he stripped out of the well-worn jeans and t-shirt he'd been wearing. Holy hotness, even with water lapping at his navel, the man stole her breath. She tried to keep her gaze locked on his but knew she wasn't successful when she heard him chuckle.

"I will never complain about appreciative looks. Contrary to what many believe, I don't believe my satisfaction hinges on adherence to the strict protocol many Doms insist upon. Knowing you like what you see assures me the attraction is reciprocal." *Is he serious?* Electricity had been arching between them since he pulled her from the attic where she'd been hiding.

After helping her crawl through the small opening in her neighbor's ceiling, Max had set her on her feet, but didn't miss a step when her knees folded out from under her. He'd caught her easily, cradling her in his arms as he ran to a waiting van. Cami remembered the rush of relief she'd felt when he first poked his head into the attic. She hadn't been able to hold back tears of joy. Dehydration from the extreme heat and muscle fatigue from remaining in one position for so long had taken a toll. When they reached the airfield, he'd carried her onto the waiting jet. It would have embarrassed her to admit she couldn't sprint the small distance between the van and the waiting aircraft.

"Let's try this." Max's words barely registered before Cami's bare ass came to rest on his muscular thighs. "Let's do a little experiment, Camila. I want to see what it takes to keep your attention focused long enough for us to enjoy a conversation."

Conversation? He's delusional. The hair on his legs was rough against the back of her thighs, the sensation surprisingly pleasant.

"If you don't stop wiggling, this conversation is going to be over before it has a chance to start." His voice was deeper and rougher than it had been earlier. The difference sent a wave of heat through her.

Cami sent up a silent prayer that Max wouldn't notice the way her body was responding. A quick look at his expression assured her that any hope she'd harbored of hiding the effect he had on her was a wasted effort.

"Umm... you said something about doing an experiment. What does that entail? What are we trying to confirm or deny?" Cami wanted to give herself a pat on the back for asking intelligent questions when her brain was scrambled.

Max was the sexiest man she'd ever encountered, and she couldn't believe how easily she was distracted by thoughts of sex. *Lots and lots of sex. Hot, sweaty, lost-in-the-moment sex that melts you into a puddle. Sex that qualifies as a gymnastics routine worthy of an Olympic medal. Swinging from the chandeliers wild monkey sex comes to mind every time I looked at him.* When his chest vibrated with quiet laughter, Cami realized she'd been thinking out loud.

She wanted to blame the stress of the past two years for the resurgence of her childhood habit, but since it was something she'd struggled with since she was young, denial wasn't worth the effort. Anytime she was so nervous that she became totally immersed in her thoughts, Cami would try to self-talk her way out of the discomfort. There was no denying her mortification. Burying her face in her hands, Cami could only hope Scotty beamed her up.

Chapter Eight

Max

MAX COULDN'T REMEMBER a time he was more entranced by a woman. She was emotionally and physically exhausted, but rather than becoming surly, she'd started chattering like a magpie intent on revealing her thoughts to anyone within hearing range. It was an unusual habit for a trained agent and one he was sure Camila worked hard to control. Only time would tell if the lapse was the result of exhaustion, stress, or a combination of the two.

Listening to her verbally sort through her thoughts felt a bit like eavesdropping, but he quickly rationalized because he was gaining so much insight. Max had never felt possessive about a woman... until Camila. From the moment he pulled her from the filthy oven of her neighbor's attic, she'd belonged to him. Seeing her standing on the wooden deck, lost in her memories, had been more than he could resist. The urge to pull her into his arms had been overpowering.

The softly rounded globes of her ass pressed against his thighs trapped his throbbing erection between her hip and his lower abdomen. There wasn't a chance in fiery hell she would miss the evidence of his desire. Camila's breath hitched, and he wondered if she was going to scramble to safety before she relaxed against his chest. Max relished the silence long enough to give Camila a chance to recenter her control but not long enough that she had time to erect mental barriers between them.

"As much as I appreciate the insight, I'll bet sorting through your thoughts aloud is a habit you've worked hard to break." He could feel the tension draining from her fatigued muscles as she seemed to melt against him, her smaller frame molding itself to his larger one. "What's the trigger, Camila?"

"Exhaustion and stress. I can deal with one or the other, but combined, they disconnect the wires to my usual defenses. Since I can't always control stress, I try to get enough sleep… but it was too hot in that damned attic to sleep."

"You've had extensive training by domestic and international agencies. I also know every training program on the planet for operatives involves sleep deprivation, so I'm interested in hearing how you got through that without spilling all your secrets." He smiled when her cheeks blushed the prettiest pink he'd ever seen.

"It would have been a lot harder if I'd liked my instructors. They considered your training inadequate unless it was pure torture." She shook her head, and he knew she was remembering the long hours, draining physical endurance tests, and challenging mind games. He was pleased to hear she'd already connected her level of comfort with her surroundings with a coping mechanism she used to work through a problem.

Knowing Camila had let down her guard enough to unconsciously talk through her thoughts while naked with him was encouraging. Hell, he'd have been happy knowing she trusted him enough to strip in front of him.

As a soldier, Max watched too many members of the military fall victim to alcoholism or drug addiction. He'd always wondered what made one person deal with stress in positive or negative ways. Camila's disconnection from her surroundings was the thing that concerned him. But he was grateful she'd found a way to sort through her thoughts in a way that didn't drain the life from her and everyone around her.

"Tell me about the Wests. I've read their bios, but I want to know what they are like to work for. Who do their friends see when they look at Kent and Kyle West?"

"Kyle is considered the public face of the club and teams, but I assure you, Kent is an equal partner in every way. Members of the team laugh about recruits assuming Kent is the softer touch." He paused long enough to shift Camila's position, hoping to relieve some of the pressure from his erection. Obviously, the distraction of conversation was doing nothing to diminish his growing attraction to the young woman whose courage impressed the hell out of him.

"I met them once a couple of years ago, though I doubt they will remember. I was undercover as a server in Madrid." Max smiled to himself because she was wrong if she thought Kent and Kyle had forgotten her. "It was one of my first assignments as an Interpol agent. I was supposed to be listening in on conversations, but I spent most of my time cleaning up the messes I made. I was the worst server in the history of servers. It was embarrassing."

"That story is something of a legend among operatives, Camila." He heard her groan and couldn't hold back his chuckle. "Kent and Kyle don't hold the encounter against you. In fact, I'd say it was a blessing in disguise since it made you memorable."

"Oh dear God in heaven. Do I look gullible enough to believe I made a favorable impression?"

Max tightened his hold on her to keep the little spitfire from launching herself off his lap. He could hardly wait to play with her at the club. Tying her to a St. Andrew's cross and teasing her with a soft deerskin flogger until she lost herself in an endorphin fueled haze was something he looked forward to. Camila made a second attempt to move from his lap but stilled when he closed his fingers over the tight bud of her nipple, giving it a quick squeeze.

"Respectful, Camila. Always respectful." She'd trained submissives, so there was no question she knew better. "It's going to take you a while to let the phony Domme persona fade into oblivion. Your soul will be more content if you are true to yourself." Before she could respond, Max got to his feet, keeping her in his arms. If he didn't get out of the hot tub soon, it would be almost impossible to make his muscles cooperate, and letting her move out of his embrace wasn't an option he wanted to consider.

Max kept his body between Camila and the security camera he knew was directed at the back of his cabin. Grasping one of the bath sheets he'd set out, Max wrapped it around her before setting her on her feet. He was grateful he'd kept his hands on her, making certain she was steady on her feet because her knees folded out from under her. Chuckling to himself, Max picked her up again and moved inside the cabin. Setting her on the small sofa, he instructed her to stay put while he moved outside to retrieve their discarded clothing. Turning off the outside lights, he took a deep breath and stared at the slow-moving water of the river as it flowed toward the lake.

Shaking off his distraction, Max moved back inside. Turning on the gas fireplace, he hoped it wouldn't take long to chase away the chill of the night air. He didn't bother moving out of Camila's line of sight before pulling on a faded pair of jeans and well-worn t-shirt emblazoned with the emblem from his last command. Walking away from a career that had become almost unrecognizable had been easy—leaving behind friendships he knew would last a lifetime was more difficult.

"Let's get you dressed before we continue our conversation." Camila's eyes were unfocused, signs of exhaustion easier to see in the lights of the cabin. "On second thought, we'll continue our conversation later." He almost laughed when she blinked several times, and he knew she was trying to sort through what he'd said. He helped her into her clothes and walked her back to her cabin. Once inside, she followed his lead into the bedroom, but stood staring at the bed as if she'd never seen one before.

"Are we going to sleep together, Max?" The softly muttered question made Max's lips quirk despite his surprise.

"Yes, but not tonight." He brushed the backs of his knuckles down the side of her flushed cheek and leaned forward to press a kiss against her forehead. Shackling her delicate wrists with his bear paw sized hand, Max promised himself he would be cautious when he finally got her beneath him. He knew she wasn't as fragile as she looked, but she was so much smaller than he was, he worried about hurting her unintentionally.

Helping her back out of her clothes and into bed, Max shook his head when her eyes drifted closed before he'd finished tucking her in.

"Sweet dreams, Camila. I've programmed my number into your phone. Call if you need anything." Her barely visible nod assured him she'd heard the reassurance he was only a phone call away. Max left a small lamp on so she wouldn't be disoriented when she woke up in a dark room. Closing the bedroom door, he moved quickly out of the cabin before he gave into the temptation to crawl into her bed and pull her narrow back against his chest.

Quickly covering the short distance between their cabins, Max was lost in thought when something on the river caught his eye. Instinctively dropping to the ground, Max flattened himself against the thick grass and activated the emergency alarm. The specialized phones were designed by McGregor Enterprises especially for operatives. Max met Ian McGregor a few years ago when he was working in Washington, D.C. At the time, Max hadn't known all the ways he would benefit from McGregor's genius.

Remaining perfectly still while waiting for backup seemed to take an eternity when he knew it had only been a few seconds. Sage McCall's signal from the corner of Max's cabin was barely visible in the moonlight. Rushing to Sage's side, the other man didn't waste Max's time with frivolous conversation.

"How did you know? Your alert hit the system a full fifteen seconds before the perimeter alarm along the river was triggered."

Max knew this wouldn't be the last time he would be asked the question. He was also confident, every one of his teammates would understand the sixth sense operatives develop. And they all understood the importance of heeding their instincts—those split-second decisions were often the thin line between life and death.

Sage's broad smile reassured Max the team had the situation in hand as the light flooded the entire compound. Sam McCall stomped to where Max and Sage stood.

"We have them on multiple surveillance feeds, and then they fucking vanish into thin air. Months of planning were scrapped in under a minute. Somebody, find those jokers. I want to know how they got away without a dozen damned cameras flashing their picture on our monitors. Maybe we can pull something valuable from this disaster after all." Stopping in front of Max, he extended his hand. As soon as their palms met, Sam's face split into a huge smile. "Fifteen seconds. Fuck me, that's a record. We've never had anyone anticipate a training exercise fifteen seconds before it was supposed to start."

Exercise?

"He thinks exercise sounds more professional since it's one of the military's favorite words. Hell, I suppose if Congress can refer to war as a conflict, we can't fault Sam for referring to one of the most intricately planned training missions we've ever planned as an exercise." Sage's laughter was nearly drowned out by Sam's snarling diatribe.

Max shook his head as he tried to wrap his mind around what happened.

"We'd planned this several months ago. It was supposed to give us an insight into any vulnerabilities in the compound's security. We wanted to reassure ourselves we have an adequate number of people monitoring the surveillance systems and enough cameras to cover every inch of the property. By the time I finish working a shift, I have a headache from hell." Sage shook his head and shrugged. "When your eyes are constantly trying to move between a dozen or more screens, it's easy to miss small shifts in the shadows." Sam looked around before and laughed. "We tried lighting the place up, but the neighbors complained."

"Seems people enjoy the dark. One fellow said he and his wife lived across the street from a high school for years and already had their fill of *those damned stadium lights.*" Sage chuckled before continuing, "Jen's diplomatic experience came in handy for that one. She negotiated a deal so complicated, you'd have thought it was the blueprint for peace in the Middle East."

Sam slapped Max on the back before telling him to get some sleep. "Bring Camila to the pool area for breakfast. The Wests wanted to welcome her, and just between us, I think they are hoping to hear what she shares with Tobi."

"Not that we're above using every tech device at our disposal to spy on them, but Tobi gets pissy when the entire team listens in on her private conversations." Sage grinned and shrugged. "We're all trying to stay off Tobi's radar. The ladies are planning a girls' getaway, and we're grappling over who is going to chaperone."

"I would think you'd be anxious to go along." Max was baffled by their reluctance but didn't miss the McCall brothers' horrified expressions. He'd seen the way Sam and Sage doted on their wife, so it seemed reasonable they would want to oversee the group themselves. Jen was also their submissive, but anyone who spent time with the trio recognized the power she wielded in the relationship.

"Not even a little. The term *trouble magnets* doesn't even begin to cover these ladies. Pay close attention tomorrow morning, and you'll see."

Sage's comment was vague enough to spark Max's interest, but he'd wait to see how things developed tomorrow morning before pressing for more information. Shaking his head, Max wondered what he'd gotten himself into. Max bid Sam and Sage good night and returned to his cabin. Stripping quickly, he hoped like hell he'd find a way to get a few hours of sleep. He was damned proud of himself for having enough control to walk away from

Camila's bed. Fucking hell, all he'd wanted was to crawl between the sheets, pull her into his arms, and keep her pressed against his chest. He'd never wanted to hold a woman while she slept; it had always seemed far too intimate. Women tended to get very specific ideas if you spent the night in their beds. Ideas about diamond rings and white picket fences. His last thought before drifting into a fitful sleep was to wonder how his world had managed to shift on its axis the moment he'd pulled a sweat-soaked woman with dirt caked to the contours of her delicate features from an attic in Columbia.

Chapter Nine

Tobi

SHE STRETCHED HER neck in a useless attempt to see over the giants sitting around her. Damn, why were all her friends so blasted tall? "In my next life, I'm gonna be tall... and skinny." The sharp swat to her ass told Tobi she hadn't muttered as quietly as she'd planned to.

"What have we told you about disparaging yourself, Kitten?"

She should have known Kyle wouldn't let the comment go, although there were times she wondered if he didn't look for reasons to give her a swat. *I swear he pounces on any excuse to have his hands on my ass.*

"I'm tired of being short. I want a do-over. Being vertically challenged is a pain." Turning to Kent, she hoped to find some measure of support. One look at his furrowed brow assured her it wasn't happening. "I don't know why you all are so grinchy. I just want to be taller and thinner. You don't know how much time I waste trying to find someone willing to get something from the top shelf at the grocery store." Staring at Kent before moving her gaze to Kyle, Tobi felt her lips thinning as she pressed them together in a hard line.

"We love you just the way you are, Tobi." Kyle's quietly uttered words made her heart clench.

"You are my heart and soul… the two of you own me, but that doesn't mean I wouldn't like to go to a movie and not worry about someone older than twelve sitting in front of me." Tobi knew she was grumbling about something she couldn't change, but she was damned tired of looking up at the entire world. Collapsing into her chair, Tobi leaned her chin on her hands, working herself into a full-blown pout.

"Darling daughter of my heart, I swear my brother and I are going to buy a cinema complex and reserve one of the theaters for your personal use." Dean West leaned over her shoulder to kiss her cheek.

Tobi wasn't sure what she'd ever done to deserve her in-laws, but it must have been outstanding because she'd hit the lottery with Del, Dean, and Lilly. Jumping back to her feet, Tobi turned quickly, wrapping her arms around Dean. Her fathers-in-law were the dads she'd never had. God only knew her own father hadn't cared for her beyond having a target for his hatred.

"You are the *bestest*." It was a hold-over endearment from when her children had been young. Kameron and Kodi West were intellectually gifted and blessed beyond measure when it came to loving adults in their lives. Remembering their fierce hugs and proclamations that whoever was on the receiving end of their embrace was the *bestest*, Tobi felt the burn of tears behind her eyes. Blinking back the emotion, she reluctantly released him when she heard the murmur of voices around them greeting Camila and Max.

Tobi was surprised to see the petite woman walking beside Max Dillon. After hearing about the Interpol agent's self-defense skills, Tobi expected to see a muscle-bound amazon who had trouble buying shirts to fit over her bulging biceps. Camila's dark hair was pulled back into a single braid trailing to the middle of her back, and her brilliant green eyes scanned the area as if making certain the patio was free of threats.

Camila and Max made their way through the buffet line and carried their plates to the table. Kent made the introductions, and Tobi could see the young woman cataloging each piece of information. Once she was finally given the opportunity to eat her meal, Camila didn't waste any time cleaning her plate before settling back to finish her coffee.

"Is there someplace quieter where we can talk?"

Tobi wasn't sure she would have heard Camila's question if she hadn't been looking at her.

"Let's move to the other side of the pool. If we go in the house, they'll follow us." Tobi knew the men were interested in hearing what Camila had to say. They would review their security feeds and replay the audio until they'd scrutinized every shift of position and vocal hesitation. Once they'd settled, Camila got straight to the point.

"The only thing I saw competing cartels agree on the entire time I was in Columbia was the need to distract Kent and Kyle West. The Prairie Winds team's efforts to disrupt the supply chain have been the most effective, and leaders of the various cartels are furious. Your husbands are damned effective, and that efficiency is costing criminal organizations millions of dollars."

"Camila, I'm not sure what any of this has to do with me. I've never been involved with the teams—not for lack of interest." Tobi spent the first years of their marriage trying to convince Kent and Kyle she could be an asset, but they'd been steadfast in their refusal to make her a part of any mission.

"The cartel's leaders rarely get personally involved in contracted work. They prefer to let the hired help do the messy *stuff*, leaving their hands pristine."

"Plausible deniability." Tobi wasn't as out of the loop as her husbands wanted to believe.

"Exactly. But this time, it's different. Their interest is not only financial but about salvaging their tattered reputations as well. This is about flexing their collective muscles and making an example of Kent, Kyle, and the entire Prairie Winds team."

As Tobi listened to Camila recount details of the conversations she'd overheard, an icy chill raced over her arms. Smoothing her hands over her bare skin, Tobi hated the icy fear moving over her. It was one thing to hear the vague warnings Kent and Kyle had given her—it was another to hear what Camila knew about the methods of torture used by the South American cartels.

For the first time in years, Tobi felt herself sliding headfirst into a well of pure panic. She could hear Camila talking, but the roar in her ears drowned out everything but the blood racing through her system. Ice-cold fear swamped her, and Tobi struggled to pull in a breath.

The pitch of Camila's voice was higher than it had been a few seconds ago. *I wonder who in heaven's name she is shouting at.* It felt like the other woman was fading into the distance. *How is that possible?* Making sense of the growing pandemonium around her was growing more difficult, and Tobi wondered if she was going to drown in her own fear. She needed an anchor... something to tether her to the here and now. The scrape of chairs on the stone pavers vibrated all around her, and Camila's calls for help sounded like echoes from a deep canyon. Kent filled her view, his chocolate brown eyes filled with patient concern.

"Breathe with me, Sweetness."

She tried to focus on his voice, knowing that it was a lifeline. When his fingers threaded into her hair, the warmth of his palm on the side of her face made her breath hitch. Sucking in a gasp of air, Tobi kept her gaze focused on her husband's face and tried to tune out the worried voices surrounding her. It took several long minutes for her breathing to return to normal. Tobi now understood why Kent and Kyle had become obsessive in their efforts to protect her.

"I don't understand how people can be so cruel to one another. Why hurt someone who has never done anything to you?" Sucking in another deep breath, Tobi let her gaze move around the patio until she met Camila's guilt-ridden face. Motioning for the other woman to return, Tobi stood on shaky legs and hugged her. "Please don't feel bad. I should have been more prepared for anything you might say. My husbands are probably grateful you have opened my eyes." Pulling back, Tobi gave Camila a smile she wasn't convinced made it all the way to her eyes. "I'm not always the most cooperative when I feel like I'm being smothered." Chortles of laughter could be heard all around the pool. Tobi tried to glare at the team members she knew had been frustrated with her in the past, but they'd all suddenly become fascinated with their boots. *Rat bastards.*

"Tobi, dear, you're too much like me to enjoy being wrapped in cotton batting. Where would be the fun in life if things weren't challenging every now and again?" Lilly West was everything a mother should be. Smart, brave, compassionate with a streak of rebellious extravagance a mile wide. She was also loving and loyal to a fault. "If those jackasses think they can torture my daughter, they are sadly mistaken."

"Lilly, dear, I don't think the boys are going to let you play with explosives again." Del West moved to his wife's side. He was struggling to hold back his laughter, and Tobi found herself giggling at his comment.

"No, last time, set the locals on their ears. Who knew there were so many young folks with no sense of humor?" Dean winked at Tobi, and she felt the flush of love radiate from her heart outward.

Turning her attention to Camila, it was easy to see the other woman's confusion.

"Lilly loves blowing things up, and she's good at it." Dean's smile ensured everyone knew he was teasing his wife.

"Most of the time." Del's muttered comment earned him a scathing look from his wife. Their antics had the desired effect.

Tobi giggled and shook her head. She sent up a silent prayer of thanks that she'd been blessed with amazing in-laws. Tobi was working for a local magazine when she met Lilly. The two women hit it off, and Lilly arranged for Tobi to interview her sons. She'd been trying for weeks to set up a meeting with Kent and Kyle, but they'd shut her down at every turn—until their mother intervened.

"Are you all right, Kitten? I'm sorry I wasn't here to help, but the phone call that I took was important. It seems our home was targeted not long after we left this morning."

"What? Oh, my God." *Dammit, all to hell, the dancing black dots are back*. A stinging swat to her ass made Tobi gasp, sending the black dots back into oblivion.

"You didn't let me finish. We're running the tapes through our facial recognition programs now. They made it into the courtyard and past the first level of security." She knew they'd set things up this way intentionally. They wanted to make certain they got pictures of anyone attempting to break in. "If we'd been home, we'd have captured them." She watched as Kyle's attention turned to Kent. "Make certain the dads know about this and that we'll be sending people over to make a few enhancements to their security system."

"Your mom isn't going to be happy if this interferes with her girls' trip." Tobi flexed her fingers when she realized she'd been wringing them so tightly, they were starting to ache. "I'll back out of the trip if that means everyone else can go." She hated to think about missing the trip she'd been looking forward to but didn't want to be the reason the other women didn't get to go. *Nobody will want me along if trouble is going to follow me to the ends of the Earth.*

"Let's table that discussion for now, Tobi. You and I both know Mom isn't going to leave if you're in danger. She's already scheduling time slots at the shooting range for her friends who aren't here, and the rest of you are headed there shortly. The man we have assigned to that area this month is already texting me asking to be reassigned." Kent grinned before shrugging a shoulder negligently and adding, "Not gonna happen. Assignments are set up months in advance, so any incidents that occur are simply the luck of the draw. In this case, the *luck* isn't anything good."

"Offer him a bonus week off if he sticks it out. God knows he's going to need it." Kyle's voice was the no-nonsense tone Tobi knew all too well, but his eyes were sparkling with a mix of love for his mother and amusement at the mischief she and her friends were well known for.

Tobi winced when she looked across the pool where

Lilly stood, slender fingers tapping furiously over her phone's large screen.

"She's such a huge blessing. You have no idea how lucky you are. Unconditional love and support are the most valuable commodity ever created. Diamonds and gold pale in comparison to what your mom gives freely." Tobi's comment earned solemn nods from Kent and Kyle, but their thoughtful expressions were quickly replaced by horror a moment later when Lilly's fist pumped into the air in obvious triumph.

"Come on, girls. I've managed to secure the range for the next two hours. Plenty of time to practice, and the smell of gunpowder is the best aphrodisiac in the world, so make sure your hot men will be home when we're finished." This time it was Del and Dean who pumped their fists, obviously more than happy to be on the receiving end of their wife's gunpowder high. Tobi threw her head back, laughing at their antics. God, she loved her family.

Chapter Ten

Max

LEANING AGAINST THE wall behind the line of women firing a variety of weapons at silhouette targets shaped like both men and women, Max was impressed with their skills. From the bits and pieces of various conversations he caught, it was clear they spent a fair amount of time practicing.

"They're damned good on the range."

Sage McCall's casual pose didn't fool Max. The man was as tuned in to their surroundings as Max was. There wasn't any way they were leaving the women under the protection of one man. Enzo Montoya was good; hell, his medal count would give Max a run for his money. No one was questioning his ability as an operative. The man was a former Navy SEAL who'd grown tired of navigating miles of red tape while the victims his team was sent to rescue were tortured and killed. Knowing innocents had died, believing their country had abandoned them, became more than the seasoned soldier could stand.

"Enzo has recommended several men from his former unit as recruits. Micah is working on their files and background checks."

Max should have expected the Wests to move quickly. He'd known they were keen to set up a second team, but he was honestly surprised to hear they were making the project a priority. Heaven only knew their plates were overflowing.

"I'm surprised they haven't tabled the project, considering the threats to Tobi."

"One of the reasons Kent and Kyle are successful is their ability to surround themselves with like-minded people. They hire smart and invest in quality people, so they are comfortable delegating." Sage turned to face Max, his expression reflecting a level of sincerity he'd rarely seen in the easy-going former Special Forces operative. "Kent and Kyle don't micromanage. They don't have to. Don't get me wrong, they're damned particular about who they hire. Kyle told me once the key to their success was implicitly trusting the men and women they hired."

Max was astonished to learn their background checks were the most thorough he'd ever seen. He knew several former men and women with a high-level military clearance who'd been screened out before they'd even been interviewed. Micah and Jax left no stone unturned.

Before Max could respond, his phone vibrated with an incoming message.

Escort Camila to the office. Use the inside entrance.

Max responded, nodded his goodbye to Sage, and moved to stand behind Camila. He waited while she finished her third practice round, smiling to himself at her perfect stance and well-placed shots. When her target returned, it was identical to the first two—the grouping so close, it was impossible to distinguish one shot from another.

Walking into the office a few minutes later, Max wasn't surprised to see several members of the team sitting around the large conference table at the far end of the room. Open folders and photos covered the gleaming wood surface. Kent West was the first to look up from the papers fanned out in front of him. It was obvious they were already studying whatever intel they'd received.

"Have a seat. Micah has put together everything we've learned to date about the cartel's operation. There has been significant movement in the past forty-eight hours." Directing his attention to Max, he added, "We're coordinating with various military leaders, but as you know, their ability to help domestically is limited."

Max smiled to himself because every one of them knew Special Forces teams operated domestically despite the mountain of red tape needed for approval. Leaders often adopted the *easier to ask for forgiveness than permission* stance when necessary.

"You're right about the movement. They aren't fooling around. Moving this many people along the border is telling. The good news is they know how close you are to dismantling their organization from the top down. The bad news is they seem to be reaffirming their commitment to striking out at Tobi."

Max noticed Camila had spoken without lifting her eyes from the information in front of her. He found it interesting how quickly she'd categorized and sorted through the thick file.

Standing just behind her left shoulder, Max hadn't been surprised when she'd pushed her chair out of the way. He looked on as Camila pulled pages and pictures from the folder and placed them in a semi-circular pattern. He hadn't figured out her thought process yet and had to bite the inside of his cheek to keep from peppering her with questions. The room fell into an eerie silence as everyone watched Camila. Kyle moved to Max's side. The former

Commander's low chuckle drew Max's attention.

"I can practically hear her mind spinning. Our daughter Kodi does the same thing. Sorts information in a way that only makes sense to her. She finds patterns where the rest of us see chaos. It's damned humbling to watch." Kyle's love and respect for his daughter were easy to hear.

From what Max had heard about the West twins, both were brilliant in completely different areas. Max hadn't met them yet and doubted they would be returning to the compound anytime soon. The private school they attended catered to gifted students, and the security systems they had in place were second to none. No one was getting near Kodi or Kameron West without their parents' permission.

Silence fell around them, and Max fought to keep his focus on the process and not the sweet scent of the woman standing close enough, he could feel the warmth radiating from her. The same clean scent he'd noticed when he picked her up before brunch was once again teasing his senses. He caught a hint of citrus but couldn't identify the earthy undertones. He made a note to ask her what she used. Maybe he'd wait until he had her naked beneath him, their bodies primed for pleasure and a level of intimacy he was convinced would surpass anything either of them had experienced up to this point.

For the first time in his professional career, Max was distracted during a briefing. Team members were brainstorming, and all he could think about was how anxious he was to get Camila out of her clothes.

Sam McCall watched him from the opposite side of the long table, a knowing look in his eyes. From the outside, Sam appeared to be all business, but Max suspected the façade hid a deep well of emotion.

"We'll reconvene tomorrow morning. If we tip them

off by rushing into this with guns blazing, we'll get the hostages killed."

Max understood Sam's concern, but furrowed brows of team members told him they were worried the cartel would rid themselves of the evidence if they waited too long. "My gut tells me we'll only get one chance to eliminate the threat to Tobi."

"The threat to Tobi is our top priority, but we don't want to forget the broader picture. Human trafficking is a billion-dollar business. These groups stand to lose a lot of money if we continue chipping away at their base." Kyle spoke from his position at the head of the table. Standing, he was leaning forward with his hands braced on the polished surface as he stared down at glossy pictures of his wife. "These pictures were taken last week. Tobi and Gracie were in Galveston checking out a vendor." The last comment was barely audible, and it was the first time Max had heard a note of fear in Kyle's tone. The shots had been taken by someone close. Max was guessing the range was only a few feet. They'd used the close proximity to prove how easily they could gain access to their target. Watching the horrors Max knew the cartel's enforcers were capable of inflicting on innocents chase like ghosts in Kyle's haunted eyes brought Max up short. It had to be terrifying to realize how easily you could lose someone you loved more than you ever dreamed possible.

"I'm with Sam on this one. Everyone needs a chance to thoroughly review the information. When we meet in the morning, be ready to put your ideas on the table. I don't care how outrageous they sound or how left of center you think the plan may look to others. Put. It. On. The. Table." Kent's words were in line with everything Max had seen about the West's leadership style. It was also precisely the way he'd handle the situation. Brainstorming was one of the most effective tools Max knew to find creative solutions to what appeared to be insurmountable problems.

Walking side-by-side out the back door, Max pressed his palm against Camila's lower back. When she turned, he took the thick file from her hands. "Let's walk through the Forum Shops. I don't know about you, but I need to clear my head before we sift through these files. Be on the lookout for a buffet table. Fuck me, there is a lot of information here." He felt, more than heard, her laughter. Damn, it felt good to know he'd been able to give her a moment of levity. Max might not have any potential as a stand-up comedian, but he did have a sense of humor.

The shops were preparing to open for members who enjoyed late afternoon shopping and early evening play at the club. Max knew it wouldn't be long before strangers were moving around the compound. He planned to keep Camila out of sight anytime the club was open to members outside the team. Screening would mean very little if someone was offered a lot of money. He was taking a big enough chance exposing her to the shopkeepers. He hoped knowing their careers were on the line would be enough to keep them honest.

"Holy crayfish and baptized kittens. Look at all these pretty pieces of... hey, wait a minute. These panties don't have crotches. Have mercy. My granny would laugh herself silly if she saw these. They didn't have anything like this at the club in... well, my previous club. None of the submissives were allowed to wear anything once they left the locker room." Max smiled when he looked up to see Camila's face flushing in embarrassment. He wasn't sure if she was embarrassed by her near slip in revealing where she'd been living or her inexperience with kink clothing, but it was endearing to watch. Hell, her face was scarlet, and her ears were bright red. Even the strip of skin exposed by the part in her hair was crimson.

Leaning close, Max whispered, "Are you imagining how it would feel to wear those panties, Camila?" There was a delightful hitch in her breathing, and the flush he'd been certain couldn't glow any brighter did. "Do you wonder what it would be like to wear those panties under a short skirt while we walked around the club? I'd make sure you were newly waxed, so when we took a break, I'd have easy access to your slick folds as you sat on my lap." Her pulse was pounding at the base of her neck, and the pace increased—the beats coming faster with each added image he planted in her imagination.

Pretending to be a Domme would have been exhausting for a woman as naturally submissive as Camila. It wasn't any wonder she was ready to switch careers. Knowing Interpol left Camila on her own for two fucking years in a cesspool was enough to make him grind his back teeth in frustration.

He signaled the shop owner to gather the things she'd shown an interest in but set aside after looking at the price. The only clothing Camila was able to bring back with her were the things in her emergency pack, but that would change today. On their way back to Texas, Jen showed Camila the private jet's oversized shower and loaned her a pair of shorts and a shirt.

While Camila took a short nap before they landed in Austin, Jen slipped him a note listing her sizes and let him know she'd already ordered a few things she knew the petite agent would need. When he'd blinked at her in surprise, the minx shrugged her shoulders before leaning forward to whisper, "Your interest in her isn't as well concealed as you might believe." Sage grinned at him over his wife's head.

"It's impossible to hide anything from Jen. To be honest, you don't have much hope of hiding anything from any of the subs at Prairie Winds. The government should replicate their communication system because it's something to behold." Sage's grin looked oddly uncomfortable, making Max think he had more experience in this area than he wanted.

"Sizes are kept on the network, so the sales staff in every shop need only access the system to deliver whatever you need. Tobi and Gracie made certain the network is available to all the clubs affiliated with Prairie Winds. Club Isola, Mountain Mastery, ShadowDance, Dark Desires, and many others can easily cater to your needs when you visit."

Max stared at Jen for several seconds before he felt the corners of his mouth twitching in amusement.

"You know there are people who might consider their system *intrusive*, right?" Max wasn't sure how he felt about sharing Camila's personal information without her permission.

"Implied consent." Max turned to see Kent West grinning at him. "When Cami agreed to stay in one of the on-site cabins, she gave implied consent to the rules of the club."

"We walk around the club without a stitch of clothing if it pleases our Dom. Trust me when I tell you, sizes are no secret." Jen rolled her eyes, the move earning her a heated swat.

"Sweet Cheeks, I swear you're never going to learn." Sage walked away, muttering about the one habit she'd never broken. Jen watched him walk away, her gaze zeroed in on her husband's ass.

"I love Sage and Sam more than I ever thought I could love anyone, but sometimes they are clueless. Rolling my eyes is my way of making sure they keep their hands on me." She sighed wistfully, and Max had the strangest feeling she was talking more to herself than to him. "I mean... look at that ass. That's some prime-cut beefcake right there."

"No offense, Jen, but the view isn't doing a thing for me." Max tried to keep the amusement from his voice but knew he'd failed when she spun around to face him.

"If there's a habit I can't break, it's thinking out loud." She shrugged, assuring Max knew she wasn't going to lose any sleep over the insight she'd inadvertently given him.

Now, Max was grateful for the convenience. Knowing the pieces of clothing the middle-aged woman set back would fit Camila properly made their time in the shop more satisfying than Max could have imagined. Spending money on a woman wasn't something Max was accustomed to. Hell, he rarely spent money on anything beyond necessities.

Smiling to himself, Max thought about the investments he'd made over the years. It was damned satisfying to watch the value of his inheritance steadily increase. A few years ago, he'd used part of the money to start a small company specializing in internet security. Little had he known how the business would grow exponentially. Kent and Kyle sent him enough business, Max threatened to work for himself rather than help them establish a second team. They'd compromised. Max would help get the second team trained, then assume the role of advisor while providing support and intel from a second location. It would be easier to secure a compound without club members wandering around the property.

Training the recruits didn't present much of a challenge since they were all former Special Forces of one kind or another. Camila would be the first exception if she wanted to sign on. She'd bring a whole different skill set to the team. Even setting his personal interests aside, Max counted a dozen reasons Camila would be an asset to the team. Pulling himself back to the present, Max watched the dark-haired beauty look longingly at a scented candle before checking the price tag and quickly setting it back on the shelf.

"Camila, if you like the candle, buy it. I've seen your background file—a candle isn't going to put you in the poorhouse."

"Cami… please call me Cami." Her voice wasn't much louder than a whisper, but he hadn't missed the softly spoken response.

There wasn't a chance in hell he was going to call her by the shortened version of her name. He already knew her friends and co-workers used the nickname, but Max had no intention of being like everyone else in her life. Shaking his head, Max picked up the candle and handed it to the clerk, along with bath salts and lotion in the same scent. Camila watched him, her gaze locked on the items sitting alongside the cash register. He could have sworn he heard her mentally calculating how much it was going to cost.

"I know I can't work undercover forever. Likely I'm already compromised for long-term missions." Max was impressed. She had a solid grasp of her current situation— no doubt that self-awareness played a role in her success. "I knew I needed to stash enough money to see me through a transition period."

Max almost laughed. According to Micha's report, Camila could retire tomorrow and live comfortably well past the century mark. Since he didn't want to discuss her financials in front of strangers, Max simply nodded. He knew the purchases would likely beat them back to his cabin.

The scene repeated itself several times as they walked through the shops, and Max was pleasantly surprised by how right it felt to spend time with Camila. He'd thought he'd missed his chance to have a life partner and family. Most of his friends were busy helping their kids plan college visits, and until the moment he'd seen Camila's dirt-smudged face, Max had been resigned to living his life alone.

Max smiled to himself as he watched Camila's expression soften when she looked longingly at the selection of frilly nightgowns. Doms loved to see their subs wear the silk and lace creations but banned them from their beds. He appreciated the sexy bits of temptation as much as the next man, but Max doubted he'd ever see anything as sexy as the shorts and cropped top Camila wore to his cabin the previous evening.

As they neared the end of the cobblestone avenue between the shops, Max stopped near one of the streetlamps. A nearby flower box was filled with bright blooms making it look like ground zero for an explosion of color. Max wasn't sure who was responsible for the compound's landscaping, but they were damned good. The specialized crews worked through the night and early morning hours and were as close to invisible as any he'd ever known. Max wondered for a few seconds if he should ask Kyle if the groundskeepers could help teach a course on blending in.

Chapter Eleven

Camila

CAMI DIDN'T KNOW what prompted Max to stop walking, but she was more than happy to take a break. Strolling through shops catering to every conceivable kink with a man she wanted to trip and beat to the floor was testing her patience. The challenge added to the strain she'd been under for the past two years, and Cami was beginning to feel like she was lost in a thick fog. Max trailed the back of his knuckles slowly down the side of her face and smiled when she blinked in surprise.

"Where were you, Camila? I know you are well-trained in situational awareness. Hell, your survival has depended on it for years."

Cami rarely blushed, but something about this man made her behave like an inexperienced teenager. *Who am I kidding? Teens today have more experience before their junior prom than you have.*

"Sorry, my mind decided to wander around unattended. You're right, it isn't something that happens often."

Max sensed there was more she'd wanted to say, but she held back. He was grateful she trusted him enough to become distracted, but until they knew she and Tobi were safe, she needed to be more aware of her surroundings.

"Knowing Tobi isn't the only one facing a threat means

you'll need to stay focused. I know you didn't get a chance to read everything in the file. Yet, you already knew there was a contract on you." That became clear the night a cartel enforcement team stormed her house. Camila's training and prior planning saved her life. The Prairie Winds team made the trip to Bogotá in record time. They'd landed outside the city ten hours after Camila's call. The flight itself took seven hours. Max smiled to himself when he remembered Kent telling the team they'd set a new response record.

"I don't remember if I thanked you, but I *am* grateful. The Wests are known for their ability to respond quickly, but…" Camila's gaze dropped as she kicked a small pebble down the lane. "I'm not sure how much longer I could have stayed in that attic. The heat was unbearable, and it was dirty… and dark." The last was spoken so softly, he might have missed it had he not been watching her so closely.

"Why are you frightened of the dark, Camila?" Max's need to understand everything about her was steadily growing stronger. The more he learned, the more he wanted to know. He wondered if she would panic at the thought of a blindfold. If she accepted Kent and Kyle's offer of employment, Camila would be required to fill out the club's paperwork, whether she planned to make use of the facilities or not. Her limit list would be made available to any Dom interested in playing with her. Max planned to be the first and only man with a personal interest who looked at her paperwork.

"I don't like it when I can't see my surroundings." Her words and body language were saying two different things. The pat answer sounded rehearsed, but now wasn't the time to challenge her. She was starting to trust him, and

Max didn't want to push the boundaries yet. Camila was a natural submissive, but she was also a trained operative. Both elements were hotter than hell, but it was dangerous to play without understanding a sub's emotional triggers.

Max moved slowly, positioning himself in front of Camila. His hands spanned her waist and lifted her until she sat on the edge of a retaining wall. Leaning forward until he filled her vision, Max shook his head from side to side.

"You played the role of a Domme long enough to know lying by omission is the same as skewing facts. My palm is tingling in anticipation, but I'd much rather spank you for pleasure as opposed to meting out the punishment you are on the verge of earning."

Max smiled to himself when he slid his palm against the side of her neck. As expected, Camila's reaction was immediate. Damn, she was perfect for him. He'd known it the moment he laid eyes on her. The soul-deep recognition of his other half was an electric jolt every time he looked at her. If he didn't get a handle on the reaction soon, his damned brain was going to short-circuit and fry his control.

"I've heard about reward spankings, but I'm not sure I believe it's possible." Max watched her shake her head and knew she was trying to wrap her mind around a concept that baffled inexperienced subs who had yet to experience two sides of the pleasure-pain coin. He could explain until he was blue in the face, but they would both enjoy it more if he showed her.

A warm breeze whispered around them, and Max could have sworn he heard a word of warning. Lifting her from her perch, Max set Camila on her feet. Grasping her hand, he leaned close, so he spoke directly into her ear as a powerful gust of wind swirled around them.

"Let's go. I don't know what's coming, but the hair on

the back of my neck is standing straight up."

Her response was immediate. A quick nod, and she was practically running to keep up with him. Sprinting around her cabin, they were several yards from the shelter of his porch when the skies opened up. A deluge of cold rain dropped in what felt like buckets, drenching them in seconds. Clamoring their way onto the wide, wood-planked front porch, Max smiled when he heard Camila giggle.

"We'll probably have to run extra laps during training for being too slow." Wringing water from the front of her shirt, she laughed at the realization the fabric was still dripping water despite her best effort.

"Strip, Camila." The command was unexpected, and she stilled in response. Barely breathing, she wondered if he could hear the pounding of her heart as it threatened to shake itself out of her chest. When she finally took a deep breath, Camila noticed Max had already removed his boots and socks. His shirt was unbuttoned and pulled from the loosened band of his jeans. Good Lord, what was it about open shirts exposing rock-hard abs and sexy happy trails disappearing into unsnapped jeans that sent a wave of heat to her sex?

"I don't enjoy repeating myself, Camila. The club's safe word is red. If you are too cold to remove your own clothing, you need only say so, and I'll help you. Your three choices are strip, use your safe word, or request assistance. What is your decision?" Pushing his shirt off his shoulders, he tossed it over the back of a patio chair and crossed his arms over his bare chest—and Camila nearly swallowed her tongue. "You should already be earning punishment swats, but I'm enjoying the way you are looking at me like I'd make a fine snack. I'll be happy to give you the opportunity to taste every inch, but first, I want you out of those wet clothes before you become hypothermic."

Damn, damn, and triple hell. Here she thought he was initiating a scene, but he'd simply been trying to keep her from catching pneumonia. Humiliation sent a wave of heat through her that had nothing to do with arousal. Camila rushed to peel herself from her soaked clothing without meeting his gaze. When she set the last piece aside, Max pulled her into his cabin. He didn't stop until they were standing outside the large shower in the master bedroom's black marble bathroom. Pulling her under the warm spray, Max gripped Cami's chin with his fingers. Using gentle but steady pressure, he forced her to meet his unyielding gaze.

"Tell me what you were thinking outside before you finally removed your clothing."

"What?"

"It was as if a light was extinguished in your eyes, Camila. Don't insult my intelligence by pretending you don't know what I'm talking about. I've already made my interest in you quite clear, and I won't stand for there to be any secrets between us."

It had been so long since Cami had been fully transparent with another person, she wasn't sure she remembered how to be herself. After all, she'd spent her entire career pretending to be someone else. The identities changed, but the charade was always the same.

His hold tightened fractionally, but it was enough to refocus her attention.

"I'm sorry my disconnection was so obvious. It was embarrassing to discover I'd misinterpreted your intentions."

"Explain." The stern tone of his voice was unmistakable. He wasn't going to accept anything less than the unvarnished truth.

"When you first gave me the order to strip, I thought you were initiating a scene." She tried to turn her face to the side, but he wasn't having it.

"Don't try to hide from me. It's disrespectful and unnecessary." Max appreciated the way her cheeks blushed beneath her golden tan. She'd spent two years pretending to be something she wasn't, and he doubted it was easy to let down her guard enough to be vulnerable and transparent after role-playing for so long. When the tension in her shoulders finally ebbed marginally, Max nodded. "Continue."

"I was excited when I thought it was a scene. It boosted my confidence to think you wanted me."

"What changed? What on earth made you think I didn't want you?" Max couldn't imagine what he'd done to make her think he found her unattractive. Fucking hell, he could barely think with so much blood pooling below his waist.

"You said you wanted me to strip before I became hypothermic. I thought you wanted to play, but you were simply concerned with my health. It's embarrassing to misread signals."

"Oh, little sub, you didn't misread anything. Not wanting you to become chilled was purely selfish. I have plans for this luscious body." Max smoothed his hands over her shoulders down to her wrists before lifting her hands over her head. Squeezing gently in an unspoken command to keep them in place, he then skimmed down slowly until his hands spanned her waist. "My plans don't include burying you under a pile of blankets while feeding you hot soup."

He felt her tremble when he pulled her close, but he wasn't sure if it was a reaction to his words or the intimacy of being pressed against his throbbing erection. Fuck, it was taking every ounce of his control to keep from lifting her against the smooth tile of the wall behind her and burying himself in her heat. He didn't step back until he felt her relax against him. The small sign of surrender was perfect. He pulled her arms back down until they rested against her sides.

"Turn for me. Let me wash your hair. I've been dying to get my hands in those waves of silk." Camila turned and leaned her head back, letting the water sluice down the length in a sensual waterfall. In Max's imagination, they stood under a cascade of water surrounded by jungle flora, the forest surrounding them alive with all the incredible sights, wildlife sounds, and sweet floral scents unlike anywhere else on Earth. Watching the iridescent bubbles of shampoo slide sensually down her long locks was mesmerizing. Damn, the woman was testing his control in ways he'd never expected.

After washing her hair, Max pulled her back against his chest and cupped her breasts with his soap-covered hands. Letting the mounds rest their weight in his palms, he rolled her tight nipples between his fingers until he felt her knees trembling. Camila's soft moans were the sexiest sound he'd ever heard.

"I'm dying to slide my fingers through your slick folds to see if you're ready for me. Pushing my cock into your heat is going to be a sensation to savor, and I don't want our first time together to be a quick fuck in the shower. We'll have plenty of time for hard and fast, but the first time needs to be a slow exploration." This time, the groan was one of disappointment rather than need. The frustrated sound was music to his ears. Finishing their shower in record time, Max helped dry Camila's hair but stopped her when she started to braid the shiny length. Shaking his head, he didn't want to be denied the opportunity to wrap the shiny strands through his fingers. Taking her hand in his, Max led her into the bedroom.

"I'm allergic to latex." Camila sucked in a breath and slapped her hand against her forehead. Her outburst seemed to have surprised her as much as it had surprised Max. "Good grief. I can't believe I blurted that out without making certain what you have planned."

Max chuckled as he looked down to where his erection was pressing like a pole against the towel he'd wrapped around his waist.

"Sweetheart, I think it's abundantly clear what I want." He smiled when her gaze followed his after lingering on his chest and abs.

"Your body reminds me of the statues I drooled over in Italy. The museums and churches there are filled with amazing works of art."

He nodded his head in agreement. Max appreciated the compliment, but he didn't plan to allow her distraction to continue.

"I know you are protected and clean." Every Prairie Winds operator read Camila's file during the flight to Columbia. Medical details were important for any rescue team. Micah Drake's reports were second to none. The details he included often made a huge difference in the way the team dealt with survivors.

"When was the last time you had sex, Camila?"

Max wasn't sure what made him ask the question. Instinct? A sense of possessiveness he hadn't previously experienced? Hell, he'd never been interested enough to ask the question of another woman. The deep rose flush coloring her cheeks was an answer in itself, but he remained silent, waiting for her confirmation.

"I haven't actually, well... umm." Once again, she tried to avoid his gaze. He was pleased when she pushed through her discomfort. Straightening her spine and lifting her shoulders, Camila met his gaze and confessed, "I haven't."

"Thank you for being honest. I know it wasn't easy." Max had never understood why, after a certain age, women considered their virginity a burden. Knowing she planned to give him such a precious gift was damned humbling. "I want you to know I'm honored to receive the gift of your innocence." This time the flush started directly over her heart before spreading outward. The significance wasn't lost on him.

"Come." He kept his tone level, but there was no question the single word was an order. Max was equally convinced Camila wouldn't miss the fact the simple command set the tone for the scene she'd expected when he'd told her to strip. Nodding once, she placed her delicate hand in his. Max relished the subtle shift in the dynamic. He enjoyed every phase of a scene, but in many ways, the beginning was his favorite because it was ripe with possibilities.

"Settle yourself in the center of the bed, please. I want to play with my gift before I deflower it." The corners of her mouth twitched before turning up into a shy smile. She moved quickly into position. When she was in position, Camila released a breath he doubted she realized she'd been holding. All the time she'd been gathering her courage, Max was focused on her body's involuntary responses. Watching the pulse at the base of her neck slow in small increments as her breathing finally evened out, Max studied her until her gaze met his. He was fascinated by the deep color of her eyes. They didn't become more intense with her changing moods. Hell, the color was so deep, it would be impossible for it to shift.

He let her wait while he studied every response. Max wasn't pretending to ignore her as he'd seen so many Doms do. Many used social isolation as a punishment, and he'd always wondered how anyone could believe the practice was effective. In all the years Max had been a sexual Dominant, he'd never seen the punishment work the way Doms assumed it would. And he'd never seen a Dom looking for a long-term relationship use the blatant abuse of trust. Period.

In Max's experience, ignoring someone simply teaches them to live without you.

Chapter Twelve

Camila

CAMI TRIED TO steady her breathing, but it was nearly impossible with Max watching her. His gaze was so intent it felt more like a caress than observation. They may not have known each other a long time, but she'd seen him in so many different situations, she felt as if they'd known each other for years. Hoping to distract herself from her scattered thoughts about her future, Cami took a deep breath and used her training to slow down her racing heart and rapid respiration.

"Watching you learn to surrender is going to be a pleasure. I promise I'll always treasure your trust. You are safe in my care, Camila." Trailing the backs of his fingers along the underside of her jaw, Max nodded when she shivered. "I'm looking forward to tying you to the bed, but we aren't to that point yet. Until then, grasp the rings embedded in the headboard." He reached past her to flip them out of their nesting places.

"How convenient."

Max appreciated her sense of humor, but since he believed in the BDSM adage of beginning as he intended to go, Max cautioned her against any further idle chit-chat.

"We'll connect after the scene and that will give you a chance to say everything you're going to hold back for the next hour or so." He chuckled when her eyes widened in surprise. "Oh yes, my sweet Camila. I meant what I said—I'm going to map every one of your hot spots. I want to know which touches send pulses of heat racing through you, which caresses leave you feeling lost and empty, and which make you recoil." Max continued to touch her, moving his hands over her arms, encircling her wrists, and loosening her grip on the headboard rings.

"I want you to relax as much as you can and block out everything but my touch. Keep your eyes open and focused on me." There was a reason the ancients referred to a person's eyes as windows to the soul. Even the most jaded person revealed themselves through their eyes. "Let's use the club's safe word. If you utter the word red, everything stops. Remember, your safe word will always be honored. If I'm doing my job, it won't be needed, but I'll never be offended if you feel the need to end a scene. Everything will stop immediately. We'll talk about what went wrong and see if we can find a way to make things work. If you start becoming overwhelmed, use the word yellow to let me know you're struggling."

"Yes, Sir." Camila's words were little more than a whisper, but like the finest bourbon, they'd gone straight to his head. Goose bumps raced over the smooth surface of her skin and Max couldn't hold back his smile.

"I'm so glad you enjoy being touched. Seeing your re-actions feeds my need and sets my desire aflame." By the time they finished, he was going to spontaneously com-bust. Using his tongue to draw wet circles around the outer edge of her nipples, Max followed the move by blowing puffs of air onto each one, watching as they drew up into tight peaks.

"Oh, God in heaven." When she pressed her lips to-gether, he chuckled.

"I won't usually ask you to refrain from speaking. This first time, I wanted you to lose yourself in the sensations without worrying about saying or doing the right thing." When he'd told her to refrain from idle chit-chat, he hadn't meant she wasn't allowed to speak at all. But knowing she was trying so hard to please him was every Dom's dream. "I had no idea how much I would appreciate hearing the sounds of your pleasure."

"It feels so good, I'm not sure how long I could have remained silent." Camila's voice echoed with relief. She was grateful she hadn't been censured for speaking.

"Can you come from nipple play?" Max was sure he already knew the answer, but he wanted to know if she understood how powerful her responses were.

"I don't know. I don't think it would feel this good if I played with them myself."

Max froze in place, shocked by her admission. It surprised him that she'd never experimented with her own body, and was even more shocked to learn no one she'd dated had introduced her to what was considered very basic foreplay among sexual Dominants.

"Teaching you all the different ways your body can lose itself in pure hedonistic pleasure is going to bring me immense satisfaction." Pressing his lips against her rapidly warming skin, Max turned his face until his cheek brushed over the sensitive area above her mound. He hadn't shaved since early this morning, so his stubbled cheek abraded the tender skin causing her to suck in a breath. "I wonder if your pussy tastes as delicious as it smells?" Slipping his fingers between her legs, Max chuckled when he found her sex slick with arousal. "You're drenched, Camila." Watching her cheeks turn crimson, Max shook his head.

"Don't be embarrassed. Knowing your body responds to my touch is fucking hot and the biggest compliment you could possibly give a Dom." It was an understatement of mammoth proportions, but there was no reason to burden her with unvarnished honesty. The truth had given him pause until he'd seen the embers of passion ignite in her eyes before she'd crawled into the hot tub behind his cabin her first night at Prairie Winds.

"Spread your legs for me, Camila. Let me see those wet folds glistening with your sweet honey." Camila pulled her bottom lip between her teeth, biting down hard enough he worried she would draw blood before she finally complied. The more time they spent together, the more confident she would become. Max looked forward to seeing her inhibitions fall away. Releasing the chains of embarrassment would let her soar. The benefits of freedom were more than she could begin to imagine.

Camila's eyes widened when he sucked a finger in and out of his mouth, the move imitating what he planned to do to her. Max slid the wet digit through the slick folds of her labia. He could already see she was soaked, but it was important for her to know when he said he was looking forward to touching and tasting her, he'd meant every word. Now that he was aware of how little personal experience she had, he was dedicated to making sure each step he took was directly connected to her pleasure. He'd worry about introducing the concept of pain and pleasure being two sides of the same coin later.

"Holy hell in a handbasket. I'm starting to understand why submissives always look like they were burning from the inside out during scenes."

Max already knew the kink club she managed in Columbia operated under an entirely different set of rules. For the most part, it was guided by the policy that nothing was off-limits except scenes involving blood or other bodily fluids. Their intel indicated safe words were often ignored by ranking members of the cartel despite Camila's best efforts.

For the next hour, Max kissed, nipped, and laved away the sting as he'd made good on his promise to cover every inch of Camila's body. When he finally reached the soles of her feet, he smiled as her toes curled before spreading wide as he pressed his thumbs against the center. Massaging her feet until he felt her start to relax, he smiled to himself. Moving up her body with what he knew was considered panther-like stealth, Max used his knees to push her legs wide.

"I'm going to fuck you, Camila. By the time I'm done, you'll know you belong to me." He planned to ruin her for any other man. The significance of being her first wasn't lost on him. It was not only a precious gift, it was also a huge responsibility. "I'm going to make this an experience you'll remember fondly." He kissed her forehead before adding, "Let's make certain your body floods with heat and desire every time you remember tonight."

Max wanted to be able to lock gazes with Camila from across the room and know this moment was flashing through her mind. He wanted to whisper in her ear and hear her gasp as she remembered the first time he pushed his cock so deep, she lost sight of the temporary discomfort. Her body would respond to the memory by flooding her sex with cream, making certain she was always ready for him.

That should make working together in the future a lot more interesting.

123

Chapter Thirteen

Tobi

"WHAT KIND OF medical scare? Damn, damn, and double damn. Nobody tells me anything anymore." Tobi's hands rested on her hips as she stared at her best friend in disbelief. "What time is it? Is it too early for margaritas? Who am I kidding? There isn't enough tequila in the entire state of Texas to fix this. I swear to St. Peter, you are making me look like the worst friend ever."

"I'm calling bullshit, Tobi. You are my sister in every way, aside from blood. All those golden waves don't mean a thing." Gracie's words made Tobi smile.

They always joked about being sisters despite their obvious physical differences. Gracie's Latin American heritage was on full display while Tobi's fair complexion and blonde hair made them stand in stark contrast to one another.

"The doctor's office called Jax when they weren't able to reach me. They told him there might be a problem with the lab tests. Those blasted tests were supposed to be nothing more than normal stuff for my physical." When Gracie didn't meet her gaze, Tobi shook her head in frustration.

"God bless, Bess. Come on, Gracie, spit it out and don't even try to lie to me. We both know it's not going to work. I know you get your annuals just before your birthday, and that's not for seven months."

Gracie winced before sagging back into her chair, releasing a heavy sigh.

"I thought I might be pregnant. I didn't know if I should be terrified or ecstatic." Gracie's stiff-shouldered shrug told Tobi neither of her friend's guesses had been correct. Tobi didn't ask for an explanation. Gracie needed a friend who listened patiently, and Tobi was determined to give her the time and space she needed. "Turns out it's early onset menopause. Can you believe it?"

What Gracie was saying wasn't as telling as her body language. Tobi wanted to curse every magazine cover that proclaimed the pages behind it held the answer to everlasting youth. Editors were nobody's fool. They played on readers' insecurities, and the cycle was never-ending. The standard they set was unrealistic and virtually unattainable by the vast majority. One of Tobi's favorite things about the kink community was their easy acceptance of others. Age wasn't an issue, and everyone recognized there was someone who loved every body type.

"Talk to me, Gracie." Tobi pulled a chair close and wrapped her hands around her friend's cold fingers. "Tell me what you're feeling." It was easy to see her friend was balanced precariously on an emotional ledge, and Tobi wasn't going to presume to understand what Gracie was going through. Medical scares were enough to unsettle anyone, and adding this powerful emotional element threatened to tip the scales. Discovering the pregnancy you weren't certain you welcomed was in fact, overshadowed when you discovered your childbearing years were coming to a premature end.

"I know I should be grateful it isn't a life-threatening condition, but…"

"But feelings are never that simple, Gracie. Knowing your body is changing in ways you didn't expect at this age has to be unsettling." Tobi reached up to brush away the lone tear snaking its way down Gracie's smooth cheek. "Don't cry. You know how I am. If you cry, I'm going to cry. And I cry ugly." Gracie smiled and shook her head at Tobi's honesty.

Tobi wasn't surprised to see Jax move through the gate. No doubt he'd been watching their interaction on the security feed. Even if he hadn't heard their conversation, his wife's body language was impossible to misinterpret. The pointed look he gave Tobi was clear as well. Excusing herself, she made her friend promise to call later so they could make plans to review a product line they were considering. She hoped refocusing on work would help defuse her friend's anxiety. If that didn't work, there was always tequila.

Passing the open door of Kent and Kyle's office, Tobi paused when she heard Lilly's raised voice.

"Excuse me. What in Heaven's name makes you think you have any control over what I do?"

"Mom, stop for a minute. You're not being reasonable. If the cartel can't get to Tobi, they'll come after you." Kent was obviously taking point in the argument, which meant they were trying the soft approach first.

Fools.

"I'm unreasonable because I won't let you control me?"

"We would never try to control you. We're only trying to protect you."

Tobi pressed her palm over her mouth to stifle her laughter. Kent's condescending tone was going to send Lilly into orbit. Her mother-in-law was intelligent, beautiful, and fiercely independent. Lilly West was also as loyal as anyone Tobi had ever known. The West matriarch was also a hot minute away from knocking her sons' heads together.

Inching forward, Tobi caught sight of Del and Dean West sitting comfortably at the far end of the office. The two men were miles ahead of their sons when it came to dealing with their wife. Leaning back in their leather chairs, the two of them wore matching looks of pure amusement. They winked at Tobi, flashing identical grins without giving away the fact she was eavesdropping.

"Kent, darling, you know I love you, but you're full of shit. You try to control me at every turn. Ignoring you saves my sanity. Look at your fathers. They know better than to try to strong-arm me. It may sound childish, but you're not the boss of me."

"Mother, we aren't asking you to cancel anything. We're only asking you to delay it or change the destination. It's much more difficult to protect you when you are out of the country. We've already alerted the other men and they are in agreement. Hell, you and Tobi are trouble magnets on a good day. Disaster is the only possible outcome if we let you leave the country." Kyle must have gotten tired of his brother's gentler approach. Tobi knew he was running his hand through his hair in frustration—it was one of his few tells, and nobody pushed his patience like Lilly.

"You tattled to the other husbands? Are you serious? Good God, Kyle, my friends are going to eat you up and spit you out. You deserve whatever they dish up. I will postpone the trip because Tobi is my daughter in every way that matters, and her safety means everything to me." Lilly paused, and Tobi could practically hear the electricity crackling between Lilly and her sons. "I'm warning you now, if you ever pull a stunt like this again, you won't like the outcome."

Since she didn't want the other woman to know she'd been in the hall, Lilly sprinted around the corner into the kitchen with seconds to spare.

"You are the daughter of my heart, but your spy skills need work." Lilly reached around Tobi to open the refrigerator. "I swear this kitchen looks like something out of a magazine. Too bad neither of us knows how to cook."

Tobi grinned before glancing quickly at the ceiling.

"The designer they hired to update the downstairs did a great job, even if he went a little overboard on the fire suppression system." Tobi suspected her husbands had a hand in the man's decision, but they always managed to distract her anytime she asked. Damn it all to dusty doorknobs, you could set yourself on fire in the kitchen and it would be out so quickly, your clothes wouldn't even be singed. "They had a similar system installed in the kitchens upstairs and in our home."

When she'd first married Kent and Kyle, they were living in an enormous apartment on the top floor of the club. She had enjoyed living in a place where she'd been surrounded by friends and staff. There was always someone to talk to, and she appreciated how the men established privacy boundaries. They'd made every effort to keep any interruptions to a minimum. Moving into the home they built on a piece of adjoining property was met with mixed emotions. Tobi agreed the club wasn't a good place to raise children, but once the kids were in college, she hoped Kent and Kyle would consider moving back on-site.

"I don't know where you went, but you were a million miles away. Don't let Grumpy Monkey One and his evil twin catch you daydreaming. You'll get the *situational awareness lecture,* and at last count, that one was up to fifty-two minutes."

"Fifty-seven minutes yesterday. I almost fell asleep. I was terrified they would start over if I dozed off." Tobi gave Lilly a cheeky grin, but her comment held more truth than she was comfortable admitting.

"God, I absolutely adore you. I knew you'd be a wonderful addition to our family the moment we met, but I had no idea how much I'd love you. You are a ray of pure sunshine when I'm balanced precariously on the knife's edge of rage." Lilly pulled her into a bone-crushing hug lasting so long, Tobi worried she was going to faint from oxygen deprivation. If she didn't take a breath soon, the black dots dancing in her vision were going to band together and pull her into the growing darkness.

"Let her go, Darlin'. She needs to breathe." Dean led Tobi to one of the barstools, effortlessly lifting her to the seat. He kept his hand wrapped securely around her upper arm as he accepted the glass of ice water Del handed him. "Come on, sweet girl, drink a little water. I swear my brother keeps our wife bound so much, she assumes everyone likes being bound—even if it's in the arms of someone who loves them."

Tobi felt her cheeks flush. *Eww. There are some things I really don't need to know about my in-laws.*

"Come, Kitten. We'd like you to look over the apartment upstairs." She must have looked confused because Kyle leaned forward and kissed her forehead. It was something he did when he saw glimpses of her innocence—something he obviously appreciated. "Rumor has it you're interested in moving back upstairs someday, and we'd like to hear your thoughts on how you see the space set up."

After they said their goodbyes, Tobi walked between Kent and Kyle to the elevator. Once inside, Kent moved to face her while Kyle stepped in behind her.

"You never cease to amaze us. You're under a lot of pressure, life is lobbing shit at you from every fucking direction, yet you set it all aside to make our mom smile. Hell, she was apocalyptic when she left our office."

Tobi gave him a smile she hoped looked more sincere than it felt. She suddenly felt like a balloon someone poked a small pinhole in—damn it, she was going to melt into the floor if they didn't stop being so damned nice. Sucking in a deep breath, she tried to steady her breathing and regain some of the emotional balance that had been draining away since she'd learned her life was being threatened.

"Kitten, we'll always be your safe haven. Don't waste your energy trying to be brave when you are scared. Fear doesn't define courage. Heroes are remembered because they use every resource available to them. History is filled with tales of those who understood the value of basking in unconditional love and support when it was offered." Kyle's words, spoken softly over her shoulder, made her chest ache as her heart clenched in response.

Tobi's mind briefly returned to a time when her life had been filled with pain and uncertainty. In her wildest imagination, she couldn't have imagined how easily love would transform her future.

"We need to make some changes, brother. When the center of our world forgets how important she is, we need to rethink our priorities."

Watching as an array of emotions swirled in his chocolate-colored eyes, Tobi was so lost in the moment, she didn't hear the soft chime of the elevator when the doors slid open. When Kent turned before stepping into the vestibule, Tobi followed when she felt Kyle's hand at the base of her spine. She'd only taken two steps into the small room outside the elevator car when the hair on the back of her neck stood up. After hearing team members comment on the silent but powerful internal warning, she lunged forward a split second before the sound of shattering glass and her terrified scream filled the air.

Chapter Fourteen

Kyle

*W*HAT THE FUCK? One second, his palm was pressing against the luscious curve atop his wife's sweet ass, lost in the feeling of her body's tempting beneath his palm, when she'd launched herself forward. Unprepared for the sudden shift in position, Kent stumbled several steps before going to his knees. Kyle knew he'd never forget Tobi's ear-piercing scream or the way she slid slowly to the floor, blood pooling beneath her. Pure, white-hot fear ripped through him as he reached for his wife.

Kent was shouting orders into the radio he'd pulled from the clip on his belt, even though Kyle doubted the directives were necessary. The shot had to have come from the cliff across the river and their surveillance system would have picked up the sound the instant it was fired. The men in the control room would calculate the trajectory and know within inches where the shot originated, and sound analysis would tell them what weapon was used.

Fear wasn't a foreign emotion. Kyle had faced it many times during his military career. But the most terrifying sound he'd ever heard was Tobi's complete and total silence. Kyle's hands frantically skimmed her. She was so utterly still, Kyle pressed two fingers to the pulse point at the back of her jaw. "Thank fuck." He recognized the whispered curse for what it was—anger-fueled gratitude. Kyle sent up a silent prayer of thanks as he took a deep breath and focused his attention on the woman lying motionless in his arms.

"I'll get towels. We have to stop the bleeding from her shoulder." Kent disappeared into the apartment they'd once shared. He reappeared seconds later with enough towels for a small army. "Thank God the bullet only skimmed her. It's a nasty slice and needs stitches, but if it hit her directly, there wouldn't be anything left."

Kyle looked to his left and shuddered at the size of the hole in the wall. He wasn't sure how she'd known the shot was coming, but he was thankful for whatever sixth sense warning she'd heeded. Smoothing the tangle of blonde curls back from her face, Kyle smiled when her eyes fluttered open. When she opened her mouth to speak, Kyle shook his head. Undeterred, Tobi's eyes filled with tears.

"Is Kent okay? Someone tried to shoot him. It was because of me, wasn't it? You're both in danger because someone wants to hurt me."

Holy hell. Kyle couldn't remember the last time he'd been so stunned by someone's words he was rendered speechless. Tobi misinterpreted his silence, assuming Kent had been mortally wounded and began fighting to move out of his embrace.

"Let me go. I have to help him. Where is he? Why aren't you helping him?"

"Sweetness, stop. I'm fine. I was unlocking the elevator and stairway." Kent knelt beside her, leaning forward to press a quick kiss to her lips. Pulling back, he stared into her eyes for long seconds before asking, "How did you know?" Before she could respond, the area flooded with people, and for the first time in his life, Kyle felt overcome with a wildfire of rage burning through his entire body.

"Ambulance is on the way." Kyle nodded and watched Sage McCall remove a blood-soaked towel and replace it with a clean one. "Tobi, God's got big plans for you, sweetheart. I'm not downplaying that damned slice in your shoulder, but any bullet capable of shattering the impact-resistant glass I know was installed up here wasn't one you want to tangle with."

"They were aiming for Kent. I felt it. I don't know how, but I just knew."

Tobi's words took Sage by surprise, and it showed. He pulled back, staring at her for long seconds. Kyle knew the other man was searching Tobi's tear-streaked face for any sign she was joking or in shock before giving her a genuine smile.

"She saved my life. If she hadn't pushed me forward, that shot would have gone through my torso." Waving his hand to where the bullet had blown out a large portion of the opposite wall, he added, "Look at the goddamned wall. It went through everything, including the stone on the outside."

"Yeah, hard to believe a shooter would be that inconsiderate. Hell, the stone is going to be a major pain in the ass to repair." Sage winked at Tobi, making her giggle at his ridiculous comment. Kyle was grateful for Sage's offbeat sense of humor because he'd calmed Tobi without missing a beat. He'd also taken her vitals and relayed them to the paramedics Kyle could hear making their way down the long driveway.

"Somebody better call Gracie. I lectured her for not calling me about her medical crises. I don't want to give her any way to call us even. I have big plans for her guilt."

Before Kyle could assure Tobi the call had already been

made, a distinctive voice cut through the chaos surrounding them.

"You had better move your ass, mister. I'm not a happy camper. Someone tried to hurt the people I love, and you are in the way. Move. You're a cutie... don't make me shoot you."

Kyle felt sorry for the newest member of their team. Enzo Montoya was quickly earning the respect of everyone on the Prairie Winds team. He'd be a valuable asset if Mama West didn't shoot him.

The poor bastard had been stuck managing a shooting range filled with Lilly, Tobi, Gracie, and several other wildcards from their group—and pulled it off without incident. Kyle would have been content if the man simply managed the group and kept the damages to a minimum and knew his brother felt the same. Supervising the rowdy bunch his mother and wife called friends without anyone alerting local authorities and without the fire department or EMS being on-site was almost unheard of. If Enzo pulled this off, he was going to become something akin to a local celebrity in no time.

"You'd better let her through, Enzo. She isn't kidding about shooting you, though I'm fairly sure she wouldn't kill you." Kyle kept his tone light, but the words were truer than the former SEAL might believe.

Enzo stepped aside, and Lilly West rushed to Tobi's side.

"I let you out of my sight for five minutes, and look what happens. I heard you saved Kent's life. Now I can see your effort wasn't without consequence. Why aren't you downstairs in the infirmary? It wasn't built for looks." Shaking her head as she looked around her, Lilly turned her attention back to Tobi. "You're sitting on the floor, for heaven's sake. The risk of infection is huge, and it's obvious the windows need an upgrade."

"She's right, and if you move her downstairs, I can close the wound. Dr. Barnes and I collaborated on the supply list, so I know there are plenty of sutures available."

Kyle was surprised to see Dr. Ben Stewart standing behind him. Ben was not only a club member, he was also an orthopedic surgeon who'd helped design and stock the on-site infirmary. If he sutured Tobi's back on-site, they would be able to provide much better security.

Once they cleared the area and positioned people on the cliff across the river, there wouldn't be any place for a sniper to hide. After a previous incident, they'd installed motion-activated cameras. Two days ago, a backhoe working across the road severed a power cable the local electric company had yet to repair. In hindsight, the timing was far too convenient.

One of the paramedics nodded to where Ben leaned casually against the wall. "Dr. Stewart is more than qualified to take care of this wound. If you are concerned about security, the last place you want to be today is the emergency room. There was a bad wreck on the interstate. A bus full of high school students on their way to a choral event went off the road when their driver had a heart attack. The bus following them stopped to help when the first tipped over. There were kids everywhere, which sent several other drivers off the road."

"All the nearby emergency rooms are filled with kids who aren't hurt and their frantic parents, who are insisting they need to be checked out. Oh… and they are singing." The younger ambulance attendant looked exhausted and amused. Kyle wondered which emotion would win at the end of the young man's shift. "The only way to describe it is *antiseptic choir hell*. It would be easy for someone with less than stellar intentions to use the utter pandemonium as a cover."

Kyle agreed. He watched as the younger man's gaze flickered to Ben's several times. *Interesting.* Ben used submission as a stress reliever and enjoyed sex with men and women. Kyle knew the surgeon hadn't been to the club in a while but had assumed the man was caught up in his career. Now it looked as if he'd found another way to fill his free time.

"Come on, Ms. Tobi. Let's get you on the gurney. We'll make sure you get downstairs and into the infirmary." Leaning down, the paramedic whispered, "It'll save your hot husbands from arguing over who gets to carry you and gets you into Dr. Handsome's care sooner rather than later." Tobi giggled as she started to stand. Weaving precariously, Kyle was grateful when the two ambulance attendants settled her quickly on the wheeled gurney. When he looked down, Kyle did a double-take at the large wheels and rugged-terrain tires. Raising a brow in question, Ben chuckled as he followed them into the elevator.

"Upgrade." Ben's response drew laughter from both paramedics.

"We get most of the lake calls and often have to traverse ground that's not well suited for regular equipment." The older of the two men nodded toward his partner and grinned. "It seems my partner is a MacGyver fan. I've stopped asking where he gets parts and supplies." Kyle shook his head when the younger of the two flushed and ducked his head.

The interpersonal dynamics were interesting, and Kyle made a mental note to check in with Ben. He and Kent tried to connect regularly with the club's submissives—

137

even those in committed relationships. Safe, sane, and consensual was the guiding tenet of Prairie Winds. He and Kent made every effort to make certain they reminded the submissives their door was always open if they needed help or guidance.

Ben put up a hand to stop Kent and Kyle at the door of the infirmary. "Wait here. The less exposure the better. She is already at risk for infection. Let's not fill the room with people and double down on the risk. It's also important for me to focus all of my attention on my patient. I don't need or want any outside distractions." Ben was one of the most submissive men Kyle had ever met, but the man he knew was nowhere in sight now.

Once he and Kent recovered from their shock, they laughed and stepped aside. Ben disappeared inside, and Kent shook his head.

"Who the hell was that man?" Kyle understood Kent's confusion because it mirrored his own.

"No fucking clue, but I hope he knows better than to pull a stunt like that in the club." Kyle knew his words and attitude were at opposite ends of the spectrum. Before Kyle could comment further, his parents stepped into the hall outside the infirmary.

"I told you a waiting room wouldn't be a waste of money, but did you listen? Nope. And now we're all standing in the hall like naughty schoolchildren sent to see the principal." She turned to smile at her husbands. "I'll bet the two of you were sent to the principal a lot when you were in school. It's no wonder our sons are so blasted stubborn." Del and Dean West both waggled their eyebrows so perfectly in synch, you'd have thought the move was choreographed.

"I'm going to the office before they go all mushy."

Kent stomped down the hall, and Kyle wanted to roll his eyes. Fucking hell. Why hadn't he thought of that? Now he was stuck standing in the hall with the only three people in the entire world he refused to discuss sex with.

Chapter Fifteen

Camila

S TARING AT THE ballistics report, Cami shook her head when the numbers and letters started blurring together on the page. She kept re-reading the same information, praying she was wrong, but knowing she wasn't.

"Wind." Cami didn't realize she'd spoken aloud until Kyle West asked her to explain. "I know you think Kent was the target, but I don't agree. The sniper miscalculated the effect of wind and temperature. It's also likely he wasn't expecting you to exit the elevator single file. If you had moved side-by-side, he'd have taken you all out with a single shot."

Collectively every person in the room seemed to hold their breath. They seemed momentarily surprised they hadn't thought of it sooner. To be honest, Cami was surprised as well since there were several Special Forces assassins sitting at the table.

"Check local hotels offering kitchenettes. He insists on cooking his own meals." Sam McCall was on his feet, moving to the door before Cami stopped speaking. With his phone pressed firmly to his ear, he walked quickly from the room.

"You don't think he's already left?" Max's inquiry was reasonable, but he didn't recognize the shooter's M.O.

Trained as a soldier, law enforcement wasn't his primary area of expertise, but Max had helped track more than one assassin. Understanding a criminal's usual method of operation was critical in taking them down.

"He would have watched for a med-evac helicopter and could have done that from a secondary observation point. The ambulance left here without any signs of urgency, so he knows there were no serious injuries." Cami hated that she hadn't been able to talk to the ambulance crew before they left. She'd been sent to a recon position on the other side of BFE and was still fuming about it. When she confronted Kent before this meeting, he'd assured her it was simply a matter of liability. Since she had yet to sign on with Prairie Winds, they couldn't risk her safety. She'd wanted to roll her eyes when he'd given her a wicked grin filled with blatant manipulation.

They'd asked her to stay after this meeting to negotiate her contract. The terms outlined in the document they'd already forwarded to her outlined her dream job in detail. After spending time with Max, signing on was a given.

"In other words, whoever accepted the contract knows he failed, and failure is not an option." Max's words were an observation rather than a question.

The distinction might seem subtle to someone outside the circle of special operations, but it was important. The man known as *The Assassin* wouldn't give up until he'd completed the mission or was killed trying. Cami intended to make certain it was the latter.

"It's obvious you've seen something that tipped you off about the shooter's identity." Cami appreciated Kyle's carefully worded comment. He'd given her an out if she felt it was warranted. If she hadn't already submitted her resignation, Cami might have taken the easy way out.

"Ballistics and angle. Chang's signature is so subtle, it's almost imperceptible. Don't let his name fool you. His pedigree is so mixed he doesn't claim any single nation as home. His last name isn't real—to be honest, I don't think anything we know about him is one hundred percent real." Cami pushed back strands of her hair that had pulled free from the thick braid trailing down her back. "He has only been on Interpol's radar for a couple of years, but there is little doubt he was active long before he came to our attention."

Kyle leaned forward, steepling his fingers in front of him to study her. The intensity of his attention made her nervous, but she was determined to hide how uneasy his scrutiny made her feel. Cami was accustomed to intimidating men and women. She'd spent her entire career dealing with people who posed more of a threat to her than Kyle West. Max moved a hand to her thigh, giving her a reassuring squeeze. The simple show of support meant more than he knew and helped her focus on her response.

"Chang is no fool, but he won't back down either. For him, it's a matter of preserving his reputation rather than a question of honor." Setting down the pen she'd been twirling smoothly between her fingers like a baton, Cami met Kyle's gaze. "I met him a couple of years ago in Madrid. I was working undercover to take down a small trafficking ring. The goal was to gather valuable information we could use to tackle larger operations."

Cami wasn't sure how much she wanted to reveal since her conversation with Chang had been a humbling experience. Taking a deep breath to steel her nerves, she decided anyone who wanted to ridicule her was free to do so… she simply didn't care.

"I was working as a barmaid, and it seems Mr. Chang

has a very specific type when it comes to women. I was paying a lot of attention to him because he was sitting near the small group of men I was watching. Much to my chagrin, he made it abundantly clear I *didn't do it for him.* No one on our team knew he was in the area, so it took me a few minutes to realize who he was." Max's hand on her leg tightened to the point where she nearly cringed. It was soothing to know he didn't share Chang's opinion.

"Seems to me, not being a killer's type would be a good thing." Surprised to see Sam McCall stepping back into the room, she was shocked to see the corners of his mouth twitch. *Holy hell, did he almost smile?* She had started to think the man was stern to the core. Someone should probably check his face for signs of cracking. Not her… but someone.

"Thank you." Cami hoped Sam knew she was sincere. Her head understood, but it had still been damned humbling. Chang's assumption that she was interested in him made Cami realize how arrogant the bastard was, and she'd enjoyed giving him a haughty look of disbelief. "It gave me no small measure of pleasure to assure him I would treasure his rejection." She hadn't recognized the young man sitting at the table with Chang. He'd snorted with laughter as she'd walked away. Cami later learned the blonde surfer boy was the CEO of an up-and-coming cyber-security organization. She'd felt terrible when the CEO was shot dead in a back alley early the next morning.

"If you were going to guess about Chang's next move…"

"He'll come straight at you because he thinks you won't expect it." Cami wanted to snicker when every man at the table stared at her as if she'd lost her mind. Jen McCall was the only other woman in the room, and her warm expression assured Cami they were in agreement. "I wouldn't be surprised to see him waltz in the front gate under the pretense of applying for membership. Don't judge him by his last name. I doubt anyone has ever mistaken him as Asian."

"While you've been talking, I tapped into our system and pulled up some fun facts about Mr. Chang. For a man whose entire career revolves around being a hired gun, he's become very careless." With a few taps on her keyboard, Jen's laptop was mirrored on a large screen at the end of the room. "Cami is right, the man definitely has a type." Scrolling quickly through the pictures she'd put together, there was little doubt every woman in Chang's company was a virtual clone of Jen McCall. Sam stepped away from the position he'd taken at the back of the room. Watching as pictures continued to flash on the large screen, he started shaking his head.

"Don't even think about it, Doll." Sam crossed his massive arms over his chest, and planted his feet shoulder-width apart, his attention laser-focused on his wife.

Cami had to give the woman credit—her look of wide-eyed innocence was an Academy Award-winning performance. Cami didn't know the other woman well, but she could spot a snow job at a thousand paces.

"Hear me out." Cami hadn't known Jen very long, but she recognized her style. The pretty blonde was going to go in easy as a first strike. She admired the effort but could have told the other woman it wasn't going to work.

"No." Sam's one-word answer was all it took for Jen's entire demeanor to flip.

Turning her attention to Kyle, Jen took a deep breath before slowly moving to her feet and leaning forward. With her weight balanced on her splayed fingertips, Jen's entire demeanor shifted. *Aww. I see the former diplomat has decided to step forward.* The woman's pose was pure power and focus. When she turned the intensity to Kent and Kyle West, Cami waited for the other woman to let them have it with both barrels.

"I thought all ideas were welcome. You've always stressed the importance of hearing every idea, no matter how crazy it might sound because it's the most outlandish plan that sparks creative input from other members of the team. As a member of the team, my ideas have always been given the same consideration as my colleagues. What's changed?"

Cami wanted to stand up and cheer. Holy hell, Jen McCall wasn't taking any prisoners, and it was clear she didn't intend to be silenced. When future generations spoke about the brave women who fought for equality, those who stood up for themselves and others, and those who kept fighting when others would have stolen their hard-one victories—Cami hoped it was women like Jen McCall who came to mind.

"Sam, I understand your reluctance, but Jen is right. We've always encouraged brainstorming. Let's hear what she has to say and let the process work the way it always has in the past."

Sam gave Kyle a reluctant nod of agreement before crossing his arms over his chest and taking a step back to lean against the wall. His body language was almost screaming *Hell No*, despite the nod of acknowledgment he'd given Kyle. Anyone who believed Sam McCall was listening with an open mind was fooling themselves.

"If we find out where he is staying—" Sam started to interrupt, but evidently reconsidered when his wife leveled him with a thunderous glare. He didn't say anything, but his growl was impossible to misinterpret. "It would be easy for me to connect with him. Give me ten minutes alone with him, and I'll have the asshat bragging about his assignment."

"Everyone knows you could sweet talk the most hardened criminal into confessing, but I'm going to side with Sam on this one. What makes you think he won't kill you once he realizes he has shared secrets he didn't intend to share?"

"What if we let Jen distract him long enough to secure the building? The only way to execute a search warrant will be to secure all the exits. The man can spot a cop at a thousand paces." Cami had seen agencies try to drop a net over the man, and without exception, he'd slipped through their fingers.

"It seems to me this plan has potential, but I have a couple of concerns." Sage McCall leaned forward, tapping his pen absent-mindedly against the folder in front of him. "I assume this fellow is no fool since he is one of the most sought-after snipers in the world. It won't take him longer than a hot minute to make the connection between Jen and his arrest. If our local district attorney is true to form, Chang will walk out of the courthouse without even posting bail."

"And when he does, he'll have an additional target." Sam snarled the words making Jen roll her eyes. "That's two, Pet."

Cami grinned when Jen's face flushed hot pink. The pretty blonde's fair complexion was probably a curse when she had two dominant husbands. Cami watched the interaction and wondered what it would be like to know you were racking up punishments. Was Jen dreading the moment she was alone with Sam and Sage, or was she looking forward to the scene?

"If you are wondering whether or not you can come from a spanking, I'll show you when we get back to my cabin." Max's warm breath washed over her ear as his whispered words sent a shiver up her spine. "I'm looking forward to our exploration. Your stint pretending to be a Domme didn't bring you any measure of sexual satisfaction."

Boy, oh boy, you're so right.

"It's going to be a pleasure to watch you come apart when you discover pain and pleasure are two sides of the same coin. Everything will seem brighter and more meaningful when your soul finds its true path."

Cami felt moisture coat the folds of her sex as she listened to Max. His words were for her ears only, but it was damned hard to focus on the conversation around her when her imagination had her over Max's knee.

"What if there were several women celebrating together in the hotel's bar?" Jen's question helped refocus Cami's attention.

"You'd likely cause a riot, but I have to admit, I think it might work." Kent shook his head and grinned.

"You have to promise you'll stick to the plan. You are not to initiate any interaction with the man. No flirty looks. No questions. No casual conversation. Any deviation and we'll yank you out of there so fast, you won't know what hit you." Sage drilled his wife with a look that made it clear he was not going to negotiate.

"Tobi won't be attending, for obvious reasons." Turning his attention from Jen to Cami, Kyle continued, "You're out as well. We won't put the two of you in the direct path of a man hired to kill you."

"Wait. What? I'm a well-trained operative. I've spent

years putting myself in the crosshairs." When Cami realized she was standing, she sat down and took a steadying breath. "I agree keeping the man distracted while you search his room will probably work. What I don't understand is how your plan will thwart his determination to fulfill his contract."

"We want to know who is paying him, and we want to make sure he feels enough pressure to make a mistake."

Cami wasn't convinced Kyle's version of the plan was going to work the way he planned. James Chang was a wildcard. It was true he had a weak spot for intelligent blondes with long legs, but he was also driven and as ruthless as the people who hired him.

Chapter Sixteen

Lilly

FINDING FRIENDS WILLING to provide a distraction was always easy. Asking her friends to meet alongside the club's beautiful pool for margaritas and snacks—also, a pleasure. Telling them Kyle would join them to explain what the team was asking them to do and who was involved hadn't been as easy.

Lilly always laughed about her friends' never-ending debate over which set of twins—her husbands or sons— were the most handsome. Unfortunately, it didn't matter how hot her friends thought a man was, none of them were inclined to follow any instruction contrary to what suited them. They'd listened politely, and Lilly could practically see Kyle's directives going in one ear and out the other.

After their poolside meeting, Lilly went upstairs to see Tobi. Her sweet daughter-in-law was recovering nicely but didn't hesitate to throw a pillow at Lilly when she recounted the meeting downstairs. Tobi threatened to throw her out if she didn't stop making her laugh.

"I mean it. Laughing is painful. I swear Dr. Ben put in a zillion stitches so tiny, they are better suited for a preemie. He said it would prevent scarring, but I've decided Kent and Kyle set me up. I can't begin to tell you how badly the sutures itch. I have to call one of them to come up and put cream on them, and you can imagine how that ends." Tobi tried to stifle her laughter when Lilly shook her head, slapping her hands over her ears. "And I'm sure Ben pulled the edges together so tight, something is overlapped because I'm continually sticking my boobs out trying to get comfortable."

When Lilly checked the wound, she understood Tobi's frustration. "Did the doctor leave anything other than antibiotic cream? Your sutures are drying faster than you are healing. Adding a layer of moisture will help." Pulling a tube of cocoa butter from her purse, Lilly went to work. Tobi's sigh of relief made Lilly's heart swell. Once she'd finished, Lilly leaned over Tobi's shoulder, pressing a kiss against her cheek. "I'll call you tomorrow to make sure you're doing better. Those sons of mine better start sorting out their priorities." Lilly knew Kent and Kyle were working far more than they should, and their personal lives were taking a direct hit as a result.

The next evening, Lilly joined her friends at the hotel where the Prairie Winds team confirmed James Chang was staying. They could only hope the man would follow his usual habit of socializing in the bar before retiring for the evening. A previous commitment prevented Charlotte from joining them, but Tabby leaped at the opportunity. CeCe sat across from Lilly, her dark hair and eyes shining despite the bar's dim lighting. Lilly's longtime friend, Suzy Quintara, was seated to her left. Suzy's background as a private investigator would help the group read the man's body language. Suzy had worked for Dante Radison's private investigative agency for years, and despite her claims otherwise, everyone knew she and Dante were a couple. Why the two stubborn born-and-bred Texans refused to admit they were more than co-workers was a mystery to everyone who knew them.

They'd made certain there was only one woman sitting at the table who was Chang's type. Jen McCall was wearing skin-tight jeans that hugged her ass like they'd been painted on. The pale blue silk blouse she'd chosen was low-cut enough to be tempting but not enough to cause the riot Kyle warned them about. Lilly laughed to herself because she knew the leggy blonde could set the entire place ablaze if she let her guard down and leaned too far forward.

Lilly rolled her eyes when she recognized the bartender, who turned as they entered. Standing well over six feet in height, Carl Phillips looked like he should be hanging out in a Southern California beach bar instead of polishing glasses in Austin, Texas. He gave them a conspiratorial wink before motioning for them to sit at the table directly in front of the bar. The location was perfect, and she nodded her thanks.

"Wow, who knew he could mix drinks? I think we should have a big party where everyone reveals all their hidden talents." Jen spoke quietly to keep from alerting the other customers.

"You might want to rethink that. Can you imagine the wild skills our Doms would *reveal*... and the imaginative ways they would choose to share the information?" CeCe's gaze was locked on Carl as patches of pink blossomed on her cheeks.

"Suzy, what's new in your world? I heard you're planning a trip." Jen's question was met with Carl's scowl and Suzy's excited squeal.

"I'm helping Tabs, Charlotte, and Lilly work on the itinerary for a girls' trip. I don't expect my ideas to go unchallenged, but I'll leave the negotiations to you ladies.

There is just one of the many reasons I have never married."

Tabby rolled her eyes at Suzy before pretending to study the drink menu for several seconds before noticing the silence surrounding her. Looking up, she noted the other women were watching her expectantly. "What? My husband died." When her comment didn't break the tension she shrugged, "What's that look about? Damn it... it's not like I killed him."

"Becoming a widow at an early age is one of the hazards of marrying a man who had one foot in the grave and the other one on a banana peel." Lilly's eyes danced with humor as Tabby shrugged off the criticism.

"Can I take your orders? We have several specials tonight." Lilly watched her friends' eyes widen when they saw Enzo Montoya standing beside their table, pen and paper in hand. He was a relatively new member of the Prairie Winds team. Most of the women and half the men at the club tripped over their own feet when he finally started using his club membership.

I swear those chestnut-colored waves in his hair and indigo-colored eyes must have had panties dropping all over the world.

Lilly remembered what it was like when her sons were in the Special Forces. Women followed them around like love-sick puppies. She'd prayed they would find a woman who saw past their looks and money. Kent and Kyle needed a woman who could hold her own against them since neither of them was prone to compromise.

"Miss?" The concern she heard in Enzo's tone pulled her back to the moment.

"Oh, sorry. Guess I checked out for a little bit. Don't let anyone fool you, getting old isn't for the faint of heart." Once they finished ordering, the group lapsed into easy conversation while they waited for their drinks. Tabby was the first to take a big gulp of her fruity drink. Her face contorted in such a grimace, Lilly hoped her phony cough hid her laughter.

Tabby leaned closer and hissed, "There's no booze in my drink. It's fucking fruit juice. Nobody said anything about healthy drinks. Somebody is going to owe me big time for this." Lilly would have been more surprised if Carl made them real drinks.

"Glad I ordered rum and Coke, at least I have a real soda. Not sure I'd be happy with a lime slushy." Jen shook her head and laughed, "I'm used to this sort of thing when we're working, but someone should have tipped you off." Jen had barely finished speaking when Lilly's ear bud crackled to life and Kyle's voice told them James Chang would be stepping through the door in three...two...

Lilly wasn't sure what she expected, but the suave-looking man sliding onto a nearby barstool somehow didn't match her mental image of a ruthless killer. She noticed he'd chosen a seat that allowed him an unrestricted view of the door... and Jen. Damn, it was impressive to see how quickly he'd taken in his surroundings and positioned himself with the best view.

"Oh, you all are the best. This was such a wonderful surprise. I'm going to miss our little get-togethers." If Lilly didn't already know how brilliant Jen was, she'd have wondered how the woman fell into character without so much as a blink. "I think that hottie behind the bar is putting extra rum in my drink. I wonder what time he gets off work. My flight isn't until noon tomorrow, so I have plenty of time to kill." CeCe shifted positions a split second before Jen grimaced. The expression was so fleeting, for a few seconds, Lilly wondered if she'd imagined it.

"I called dibs on him first. Just because you're moving across the country doesn't mean you don't have to play by the rules." CeCe might have been speaking to Jen, but she'd never taken her eyes off Carl. Playing their roles perfectly, Carl gave his lover a panty-melting wink and blew her a kiss.

"Well, damn. Did you see the size of his hands?" Fanning her face with a napkin, Jen looked ready to swoon. Lilly wondered how deep the pretty woman was going to dig her hole before she settled down. "I'm already imagining what it would be like to have his hands skimming over my bare skin." Lilly could have sworn she heard a man snarl in her earbud. "You know how much I like... well, *sex.*" Lilly laughed as Jen pretended to whisper the last word. Damn, the woman missed her calling... she'd have made an amazing actress. Everyone who knew Jen knew she only had eyes for Sam and Sage, but the woman drew people to her like a damned magnet.

Chapter Seventeen

Cami

C AMI SAT IN the hotel's cramped security office, scanning the bank of monitors as Jen McCall captured Chang's attention before he walked into the bar. Seeing the way Chang zeroed in on Jen from the hotel's lobby made Cami nervous. Knowing Jen was willing to have a huge target painted on her back spoke volumes about the Wests' team. The men and women who joined the Prairie Winds team acted more like family than colleagues.

"She saw him in the lobby. Jen McCall's situational awareness when she is working is something to behold." Cami knew Kyle was speaking to her, but he hadn't taken his eyes off the bank of monitors. "Jen's diplomatic training has served her well."

"The fact her I.Q. is off the fucking chart doesn't hurt either." Cameron Barnes's obvious respect for Jen made Cami smile. Cam knew better than be seen in the bar. There wasn't an agent or hired gun in the world who wouldn't recognize him on sight. Cami couldn't deny being a little star-struck sitting next to him. The man was practically a legend among the agents she'd trained with. "It's remarkable if you think about it. Prairie Winds is the social hub for a group of women who are each remarkably intelligent in different ways. Every one of them has a different type of intelligence, and they balance each other in ways the club's Dominants watch in wonder."

Cami leaned forward when Chang asked Carl a question. "Have they been here long?" She had to give him credit; James Chang was damned slick. She'd bet her last nickel he knew exactly how long the group had been in the bar. Every piece of intel she'd read on the man said he rarely asked a question unless he already knew the answer. Carl glanced at the group of women and shrugged without answering. "Are they regulars?"

"I wouldn't call them regulars, but I've seen them here a time or two. They always have a good time and never cause any trouble." Carl's comment made Kyle's mouth drop open and Cam stood nearby shaking his head. Cami couldn't hold back her soft laughter. She hadn't been at Prairie Winds long, but Cami knew enough to worry Carl was in danger of being struck by lightning. It seemed she wasn't the only one who'd caught Carl's exaggeration.

Cam sighed, "And he has always been so honest. Hell, he's usually honest to a fault."

"That comment alone could blow the whole operation. Who could look at that group and not see trouble?" Cami could hear the amusement in Kent's voice.

Smiling to herself, Cami was starting to understand the different communication styles, and found herself relaxing. The group hadn't left all the military protocol behind, but it seemed they'd learned to appreciate the joys of family and friendship.

Cami looked on as Chang approached the table where the women were enjoying their virgin drinks. You'd never know those drinks didn't have an ounce of alcohol in them. *If they are this wild without any booze, I wonder how wild their parties are when their drinks are made correctly.* It didn't escape her attention when Chang positioned himself, so he was directly across from Jen.

Cami was fascinated by the man's body language and unconsciously tuned out his words for a few seconds. His moves were well practiced and so smooth it would have been difficult to spot his intention if she hadn't already known he was interested in a set of very specific physical characteristics in women. Chang's relaxed approach belied the intensity and focus she saw in his eyes.

"Hello, ladies. I'm in town on business. Would it be all right if I pulled up a chair? You seem like you're having a great time, and I could use a little laughter."

"Well, bless your heart. You having a bad day, sugar?" Tabby gave him a sympathetic look, but even Cami knew *bless your heart* was Southern woman code for *fuck you.*

"Yes, ma'am. To be honest, the whole week has been a challenge."

"What kind of business are you in, Mr...? Oh, dear, I'm sorry. I didn't catch your name." Lilly was so polished, you'd have thought she'd been sculpted from Italian marble.

Cami wondered if Kent and Kyle knew what an untapped resource they had within their reach. The team searching Chang's room was nearly finished. According to the background chatter coming over her earbud, there wasn't much to see. No laptops. No weapons. Not so much as a scribbled note for Door Dash.

"I fix problems. I work independently and travel light. It makes it less interesting for anyone breaking into my room." He hadn't told them his name and something about his words made the hair on the back of Cami's neck stand on end.

"Fuck. He knows. Get them out of there." Kyle's voice

was loud enough through her earbud it made Cami flinch.

"Wait." Cam shook his head. "If you pull them now, you'll prove his suspicions right. Let this play out a little longer. Search the adjoining rooms and those directly above and below the one you tagged as his." Cam Barnes' voice never fluctuated as he watched the monitors. He was studying the situation, but his gaze continually zeroed in on his wife. "Jen, let's dial things up, shall we?"

To her credit, Jen McCall didn't betray even the barest hint of emotion. You'd never know she'd been given the go-ahead from a man whose reputation as a strategist was legendary. Her men on the other hand, weren't as pleased. Cami was certain she heard the distinctive sound of snarling over her communication device. The only question was how many members of the team disagreed with Cameron's orders to expand the search and for the ladies to continue distracting Chang.

"Do you live in Texas? You don't sound like a Texan." Tabby's question sounded innocent enough, but her eyes were dancing with devilment. It was easy to see why she and Lilly were friends.

Cami hadn't gotten to spend much time with Lilly, but they did have a brief conversation the day before. Lilly had given her a bone-crushing hug and reminded her of the importance of being true to herself.

"And don't forget to be outrageous. You need to start when you are young so the shift as you age doesn't set off alarms. The last thing you want is to be stuck in a special unit in a hospital you can't leave just because you were playing." Her lilting laughter had drawn smiles from Dean and Del who were standing across the room. Cami understood why everyone who mentioned Tobi West commented on her love for her in-laws.

Pulling her thoughts back to the scene playing out on the monitors, Cami watched Chang continue to deflect the ladies' inquiries.

"No, I'm here for business." Chang's answers were becoming much more clipped, and he was obviously distracted by his phone.

"Me, too, I'm leaving tomorrow morning and felt like celebrating with my friends." Jen's perky voice was enough to pull Chang's attention away from his phone, which had no doubt been her plan. "They all have to work early tomorrow morning and are threatening to abandon me. Can you believe it? What a bunch of party poopers." Cami shook her head. Jen McCall would make millions as an actress.

"If she thinks she's going to be alone with a paid assassin, she better think again." Sage snarled his displeasure from his seat near hers making Cami wonder which brother was the most protective. She didn't have to wonder for long.

"I'm going to paddle her ass. She won't be able to sit for a damned week." Sam's threat sounded too real—even though she'd only heard it over the small communication device.

Cami had met most members of the Prairie Winds team and though he wasn't the largest, she found Sam McCall the most intimidating. Max's hand moved to her knee. The warmth of his palm and the reassuring squeeze he gave her was a show of support she hadn't realized she was missing. Cami had worked alone for so long, she'd forgotten how good it felt to have someone in her corner.

"When this is done, I want you to spend some time with the McCalls. I'm convinced you have gotten the wrong impression of Sam."

Cami nodded her agreement but wasn't convinced. The man scared her, and she was rarely afraid of anyone. Taking a deep breath, Cami tried to refocus on the monitor in front of her when she noticed Sage in her peripheral vision.

Sage gave her a reassuring smile before tapping the device in his ear, silencing whatever he was going to say. She wasn't sure what was on his mind that he didn't want the rest of the team to hear.

"Sam's a protective bastard. He's loyal to a fault. Too damned honest most days. But there is no one I'd rather have at my back. And don't let his gruffness fool you. Jen owns him, the same as she owns me. Do you think a woman like Jen would submit to a man like Sam unless she felt completely safe?"

"No, I guess not." Cami felt some of the tension drain from her muscles as she started to relax. "He reminds me of someone, but I'm having trouble piecing it together. I feel a vague sense of danger when I hear his voice, but I don't know why." There was something buried in her memories that triggered the fear, but she couldn't pull the elusive information to the surface.

"Aren't you a sweetie? I appreciate you offering to stick around and chat with me after my friends leave. It's hard to believe they are bowing out."

"Wait. If you're going to keep Jen company, we need to know more about you. After all, you could be a serial killer. Just because you're good-looking doesn't mean you're a good person. Remember that young man who drove the VW bug? What was his name? He was a looker just like this fellow." Suzy spoke up, deliberately slurring her words and doing a bang-up job of appearing drunk when the group's drinks were all virgin. Cami saw Dante

Radisson straighten from his position at the back of the room.

I wonder what the story is between those two.

"While you all interview Mr... Oh, damn, I still don't know what to call you." Jen was on her feet, teetering in her heels as she leaned against the back of her chair. Cami instinctively knew what the other woman was planning and laid her hand over Max's forearm in warning.

"She's trying to lead him away from the others. Jen has seen something that's alarmed her." Before Max could respond, Sam McCall's voice came over her earbud.

"We found it. Good call, Cam. We bypassed the first level of his security but didn't want to risk taking time to tackle every layer of his system. He has been alerted, and we need to pull the ladies out. Now."

Cami was already moving to the door when her feet were suddenly dangling several inches above the ground.

"Where do you think you're going, Camila?" Max's question sounded more like a warning than an inquiry. Fucking hell, she wasn't used to being sidelined simply because a target might recognize her. "You think Chang will hesitate to make an ordered hit in public? Tobi isn't the only target, Camila."

"I can't let them get hurt. I won't be able to live with myself if they are hurt in my stead." Cami hated the way her voice shook. She was supposed to remain detached, damn it. She wasn't supposed to react emotionally. She was too well trained to let her personal feelings come into play.

"Let the operators do their job." Max's words were a stark reminder that she hadn't officially signed on. She'd requested a couple of minor changes to the contract Kent and Kyle presented her and was waiting for a clean copy before signing.

Max loosened his grip enough to let her slide back to the floor. There was no way she could miss the feel of his rigid erection moving slowly from below her ass to settle against her back. How on earth could he be hard now? Things were going to hell in a handbasket, and he was making absolute certain she knew how much he wanted her. Laughing to herself, Cami wondered if it was the epitome of unprofessional or a huge ego boost for her.

"Get back to your seat, Camila, before you get a pad-dling to match Jen's." She wasn't sure if the threat was real, or he was simply trying to distract her. "I see the question in your eyes, little warrior. Don't think for a minute I won't punish you for not taking proper care of what I consider mine."

Returning her attention to the monitors, Cami forced herself to focus on what was happening in the bar rather than letting her imagination run wild. She still wondered if Max's threats should be insulting or send her up in flames.

CeCe and Lilly stood at the same time and burst into giggles as if it was the funniest thing in the world. Leaning against each other, the two of them motioned for Tabby to join them. "Come on, Tabs. If Jen's going to the powder room, it's our response... um, no. Reprieve... no. Shit, that's not right either." Lilly was weaving and leaning so far to one side, Cami was worried she'd topple over.

"Responsibility. That's the word you are looking for. Damn, my parents are going to be happy to learn all those years of college are paying off." CeCe's grin made Cam shake his head and chuckle.

"Every damned time we let her help on a mission, she proves how brilliant she is. If Hollywood had found her first, a lot of patients would have suffered needlessly."

Camila looked at Cam Barnes to see if he was serious. The group was in danger, and his observation was about his wife's acting ability? Seriously?

"You think awfully loud, agent. Look closely at Carl."

When had Carl stepped from behind the bar? The man was damned fast on his feet. Both women leaned against him as if he was the only thing keeping them on their feet. They'd only taken one step before the unmistakable sound of a gun being cocked sounded in her earbud.

Chapter Eighteen

Max

THE INSTANTLY RECOGNIZABLE sound of a bullet being chambered put the entire team on alert. The group searching Chang's room finished cloning his computers and backup phones. It had only taken a minute to scan the few documents they found. They made certain they'd finished before they notified local authorities because no one held much hope law enforcement would share information relevant to a pending investigation. The team didn't have the authority to take the bastard out since there wasn't an "imminent threat"... until he'd pulled a weapon.

"Don't take another step." Chang's voice was full of malice as he pressed the barrel of his weapon against Jen's ribs.

"You don't want to make this mistake, Mr. Chang." Chang didn't react to her use of his name—something he hadn't provided. Watching Jen's knowing smile was the only warning Chang had before she slammed him to the floor. Max blinked, and it was over. The man's gun clattered to the floor several feet from where she pressed a high-heeled shoe between his shoulder blades. Jen kicked the weapon well out of his reach. Pulling her foot back, she kicked Chang in the ribs. The pointed toe of her shoe elicited a groan from Chang and a snarl from Jen.

"Pull a gun on me? You're an asshat. You tried to shoot my friend because some hooligan paid you? You're a criminal. Boy, you really take the cake. You think you're slick, but I saw the outline of your gun. You're a jerk... and a wimp now that you don't have a weapon. Look at you facedown on the floor, whining like a pansy-ass." Max could hear laughter all around him as team members moved into place. When she pulled her leg back to kick Chang again, Sam wrapped an arm around her torso, effortlessly lifting her into the air.

"Good work, Pet. Let's keep the bodily damage to a minimum. I'm sure the Feds have questions for Mr. Chang."

"They can start with what makes him think any woman would fall for his bogus bullshit lines. Most middle schoolers talk a better game. Prick lips piece of pond scum."

"Language, Doll." Max shook his head and chuckled at McCall's response. The man may have sounded unyielding, but the corners of his mouth were twitching in amusement.

Dean and Del were escorting Lilly and Tabby out of the bar, much to the women's annoyance. Dante was standing toe-to-toe with Suzy, and Max would love to hear that exchange.

"Listen, you can boss your wife around, but I'm happily single, so—" Before Tabby could finish, Del turned to her and frowned.

"The fact you don't have someone making certain you don't waltz into the devil's playground is exactly why my brother and I will make certain you get home safely."

"Home? Oh, no. The valet can bring my car around, and I'll be on my way."

Max cringed and nudged Cami.

"Watch Del. You're about to see his entire demeanor turn on a dime." Max felt Cami shift in her seat to get a better look.

"Tabby, we've known each other most of our lives, so you know better than to believe I'm going to let you drive home alone. Now, be a good girl so I don't have to paddle you right here in front of God and everybody." There was an audible gasp around the room since every member of the team heard the exchange.

"You have always been pushy, Del West. I swear I don't know why Lilly puts up with you."

"He's really good in bed, Tabs." Lilly giggled as she stepped away from Dean to give Del a chaste kiss. "Come on, hot stuff. The sooner we get Tabby home, the sooner we can get naked."

Several team members giggled as Kent and Kyle groaned.

"Damn, I really didn't need to hear that. I swear she is turning into a sex-crazed senior citizen. It's embarrassing." Kent's comment made Lilly grin.

"Embarrassing your children is a privilege earned by mothers. We carry you around for nine months while you tap dance on our bladder, then our bodies push you out of a spot that wasn't made for melon heads. Believe me, we've earned the right to make you uncomfortable." She turned to Dean, returning his smile. "You and your brother made me forget about all those hours I spent in labor, didn't you, handsome?"

"You bet your pretty ass, we did." Turning to Tabby, Dean waggled his eyebrows. "We'll send someone for your car, Tabs. Now come along like a good girl, so we can get home. We've got big plans for our sweet subbie." This time the chorus of groans was louder, making Max laugh out loud. The Wests knew they had an audience and were working the room like pros.

Agents entered the bar quickly taking Chang into custody, and Camila leaned back in her chair to stare at the ceiling.

"He'll be out in under an hour. He'll have to make his way to his stash because we all know what they found is the tip of the iceberg."

"We're counting on it, Camila." Cam Barnes reached up to tap the mute button on his earpiece and nodded his head to them, indicating they should do the same. Turning his chair to focus his attention on the woman sitting beside him, he said, "I know you are new to private work, so let me enlighten you. We'll know the moment he hits the street. Everything is in place, and Chang won't be able to fart without us knowing it."

A slow smile spread over Camila's face, and Max struggled to hold back his laughter.

"Lightbulb." Cam shook his head, rolling his eyes. "Sorry. My kids watched that damned movie until I wanted to buy every DVD in the city just so I could blow them up. I swore I was going to enlist Lilly's help. She loves a good explosion." He must have noticed Max's confusion and explained, "The movies with those little yellow fellows. Minions. I have to admit, I kind of liked Gru, but..." Glancing back at his screen, Barnes did a double-take. He'd started to get to his feet but quickly settled back into his seat. Using the dual joystick controls, he zoomed in on three people making their way from a dimly lit corner.

"Well, I'll be damned." When he tapped his earbud to unmute it, Max and Camila did the same. "You never cease to amaze me, Kyle. And don't think for a minute I don't know it was you who made certain our local photojournalist was seated nearby."

Max and Camila looked at each other and nodded. "I didn't know Mia Mendez lived in Austin. I've met her several times over the years, and I can tell from Camila's response she has as well. She does incredible work."

"She has a knack for capturing nuances everyone else misses." Sage was right. Mia's shots would be helpful.

When they finished gathering the team's equipment, Max and Cami helped him carry everything out of the small office, thanking the security team for the use of their facilities.

"I'm sure Kent and Kyle will be in touch." He gave the men a sly grin and winked. Negotiation is your friend, fellas." The hotel's staff laughed and nodded. Max got the impression they would use the information wisely.

Since Chang was already in custody and on his way to the local FBI office, Camila was allowed to enter the bar. They'd been careful to conceal her entrance through the same side entrance Cam used when they arrived. Max teased her when she wound her hair atop her head and secured it with a baseball cap.

"You look like someone's little sister." When she narrowed her eyes, he laughed, "Seriously. You look twelve. Someday, you'll be thrilled with that compliment."

"Why, how old are you?" He forgot she didn't have access to his bio yet. Once she signed with Prairie Winds and her membership application for the club was approved, Camila would be surprised by the information she had at her fingertips.

"I will be thirty-eight in September." He looked down, giving her a lopsided grin. "I know how old you are, Camila. I believe I mentioned earlier, we have complete bios on anyone we are sent to pull out of a steaming attic." Her eyes went impossibly wide for a fraction of a second before she burst into a fit of giggles. Max was surprised at how much he enjoyed the sound. Everything he'd learned about Camila indicated her life hadn't been a barrel of laughs.

"Hey, girl. How ya doin'? Jen moved quickly across the room to pull Camila into a hug. "We didn't get to shoot the sorry bas...s player," but I got a few good licks in before Sam made me quit." She cast a furtive look over her shoulder to where Sam stood, shaking his head. Sage moved to her side, wrapping his arm around Jen's shoulders and pulling her close.

"Baby, it was a hell of an effort, but I'm not sure *bass player* was the save you needed." Max heard the amusement in Sage's voice and chuckled as the man whispered something else in her ear. He hadn't heard what Sage said, but Jen's cheeks turned a lovely shade of pink, so it must have been one hell of a sexual promise... or threat.

Cameron Barnes walked behind the bar like he owned the place and pulled his wife into his arms, giving her ass a sharp slap. "You never cease to impress. I'm looking forward to rewarding you, but first, Kyle wants everybody back in his office to debrief."

"Micah can hardly wait to get his hands on the hard drives we cloned," Sam added. "The man lives for this sort of thing. He's probably rubbing his hands together like a mad scientist in anticipation. Let's hope he finds what we need to neutralize the threat to Tobi and Camila." The older McCall brother was already moving toward the back exit with his hand wrapped around Jen's upper arm. His long legs were eating up the distance, his pace so fast he was practically dragging her along beside him. Their height difference gave him a distinct advantage, and he wasn't bothering to slow his steps to make it easier for her.

An hour later, they'd filled in the blanks for Kent and Kyle. There hadn't been much they could add since the men had watched multiple video feeds. Max knew the men well enough to know they hadn't missed a thing.

"Before we wrap this up, I want to reiterate, Tobi, Cami, and now, Jen, are to stay inside the secured perimeter of this compound unless they are accompanied by an armed team member. Chang will likely be out on bond before midnight unless they can convince a judge hold him longer, which won't be easy with his connections."

If Kyle thought he could slip in his restrictions without Cami noticing, Max thought the man needed to reconsider. When he felt her stiffen beside him, he gave her a stern look, letting her know this wasn't the time to voice her objection.

"We'd like to formally welcome Camila to the team. We received her signed contract just before this meeting."

That was news to Max. While he was relieved she'd finally formalized her decision, he wasn't thrilled she hadn't shared the information with him beforehand. Maybe a half-hour over one of the spanking benches in the club's main room would help her remember she'd agreed to give submission a shot.

Max had known it wasn't going to be easy for her, but he hadn't expected problems this soon. Camila might think she'd spent the past two years pretending to be someone she wasn't, but in reality, Max suspected it had been much longer. Everything he'd learned about Camila made him realize she'd spent her entire life fending for herself.

Cam Barnes had shaken his head when he told the team that she'd excelled as a trainee and despite an aptitude for electronic communication, when the Agency transferred her to Interpol they listed her as a field agent adept at long-term undercover intelligence gathering. Kyle West had shaken his head and muttered, "Typical." It didn't take a rocket scientist to figure out the Agency was covering its own ass. Camila obviously knew enough about their methods of operation to provide Interpol more than the CIA was willing to share.

"Camila, I know you had hope to return to Virginia to wrap up things at your apartment, but under the current circumstances that isn't possible. So, we've arranged for a moving company." Before Kent could finish, she started shaking her head.

"They'll never find everything, and if they do, it won't be safe for them to travel with the documents." A few team members who'd stood when the meeting appeared to have taken a personal direction, sat back down, their attention darting from the Wests to Camila. "What I mean is... I've got a go bag stashed behind a fake wall most people will never see. There is a satchel of computer storage devices beneath the floorboards." Her cheeks turned pink, and she was suddenly awfully interested in her hands clasped twisting on the table in front of her.

"How much in your apartment is yours, Camila." Kyle's question didn't surprise Max. He'd been wondering the same.

"The clothes and a few personal items. Two, maybe three boxes, along with the two bags. The bags are locked but could be broken by a professional. My goal was to keep out petty thieves and amateurs who wouldn't understand the significance of the contents. I know it would be impossible to keep professionals from gaining access to the evidence I've been gathering." Pausing for a few seconds, Camila appeared to be considering how to proceed. "As

I'm sure you are aware, a small group of the world's richest people have a specific political and economic agenda." She took a deep breath before continuing. "I was relegated to undercover work because I was getting too close to putting together enough information to shine a bright light on their activities."

For the first time since he'd met him, Max could honestly say Cameron Barnes seemed surprised. Turning away from Camila, Cam spoke to Kent and Kyle.

"Send three people, but only one enters the apartment—the other two cover the building's exits. Fly privately, but don't use your own aircraft. Keep this completely dark. Burner phones and nothing online."

"Agreed. Camila, you'll brief the team before they depart. Now, let's get outside before my mother and wife start in on us about ruining the feast they've set up for you." Kyle's entire expression changed at the mention of the two women.

"Welcome aboard, Cami. It's going to be a pleasure working with you." Sam McCall gave her a respectful nod as he got to his feet. "Anybody who can surprise Cam is going to be fun to have around."

Cam's glare was all it took to break the ice. The room erupted into raucous laughter, followed by every member of the team stopping to introduce themselves and welcome Camila to the team. Hell, they hadn't done that for him when he'd been introduced to the group. When things finally settled down, Max turned to Cami and sighed.

"I can't decide if I should congratulate you or paddle your ass." Her eyes widened in surprise, and nearby laughter made her cheeks flush with embarrassment. It was remarkable she was still easily embarrassed after everything she'd experienced in South America. Max didn't want to think about the types of things she'd seen in the club she managed. The establishment didn't seem to have many rules and members of the local cartel weren't known for their high moral standards when it came to caring for their sexual partners.

Kyle smiled at them and said, "That discussion needs to be tabled. Have something to eat and let us welcome you to the group. Tobi is anxious to talk to you. She's the ultimate welcoming committee and will be hurt if the two of you don't attend. God only knows how she knew we'd get your contract today. The woman's timing always slays."

"Camila signing her contract today was news to me as well." Max didn't try to hide his frustration.

"I wanted to surprise you. I thought you'd be pleased." Camila's response was simple enough, but Max hated the fact she wouldn't look him in the eye.

"I'm pleased with the contract, not with the surprise." Max was trying to rein in his temper. Camila was a natural submissive who'd been independent her entire adult life. It wasn't going to be easy for her to adapt.

"Cami, why don't you go out to the party? I know Tobi is anxious to talk to you. I want to discuss location ideas with Max for a few minutes."

Max sensed there was more to it than Kyle was saying, but nodded his head in agreement. He was as anxious as the Wests to get the new team set up. As soon as they were alone, Kyle motioned for Max to follow him. Once they'd entered the office, Kyle pulled two bottles of water from the small fridge and switched on the large wall mounted screen. Max settled in—it looked like this chat was going to be more involved than he first anticipated.

Chapter Nineteen

Kyle

*T*OO BAD IT'S *so blasted early. I'd much rather be drinking beer than water.*

It was painful to watch Max head down the wrong path with Camila. His interest in her has been obvious since the moment he pulled her from the attic. The former major had seen past the sweat and grime. Between one heartbeat and the next, he'd claimed her as his own. It was easy to see Camila was attracted to Max as well... but she was a fraction of a second from running.

"We originally considered locations in or around the Black Canyon in Colorado. We had a few options but there are inherent problems with each locale. In order to get a parcel large enough and flat enough for a runway, we'd be forced to buy in a narrow space between mountains. Not ideal for several reasons."

"Difficult to defend when you're trapped in a narrow space with sheer rock walls boxing you in on both sides." There was a reason terrorists used caves and tunnels high in mountains. Great defense and the damned things had been there for centuries. Replicating that in the Rockies would require years to complete and that was if you could get the mining permits, which was doubtful.

"Utah is out because the locations we were interested

in were in or adjacent to national parks." Kyle couldn't hold back his laughter. He didn't think there was any place in the entire state where they'd be welcome.

"Kansas?" Max wasn't familiar with the Sunflower State, but he knew there were plenty of wide-open spaces.

"Oddly enough, the most ideal locations were too close to Fort Riley, McConnell Air Force Base, and a place called the Smoky Hill Bombing Range. It isn't what it sounds like, but it turns out the nearby airport is a former Air Force Base in Salina. Their airport runway is next level. It's a second or third backup landing runway for the Space Shuttle. Too bad they don't want to sell it. That damned runway is a thing of beauty." Max appreciated Kyle's off-beat sense of humor. Their past military careers gave them a unique perspective.

"So far all I've heard is about the places you've scratched off the list. I know you don't want a place that gets a lot of snow." Max wanted to hurry along the conversation, anxious to get Camila back to his cabin.

"We don't mind training in the snow occasionally, but it's not an option for a second facility. We have found a place, but we haven't approached the owners yet." Something about Kyle's tone sent up warning flags for Max. "The land across the river would be ideal if we could acquire acreage flanking it."

"How much acreage are you looking for?"

"Two long sections on each side." Max must have looked as confused as he felt because Kyle chuckled. "Sorry, sometimes I forget not everyone grew up hearing farming and ranching lingo. Because the road cuts the sections in half, we want two of those end-to-end on each side. That means we'd have a property that ran a full three miles along the road and a half mile deep. We wouldn't put up a fence along the river to keep from drawing the ire of boaters who won't want to look up and see razor wire. We would install a variety of sensors in the rock cliff and under the ground along the edge."

"What are the chances you'll be able to buy the land you want?"

"It's not a question, really, but we'll be using strawmen to shield our identity. If word gets out that we are land shopping, the prices will skyrocket. It would be worse if the dads tried to help since they already own the property in the middle." Max remained silent and waited patiently for what he was convinced was coming. "We'd like you to buy one section. We're going to ask Enzo to purchase the other. We need names none of the locals will recognize."

"I assume these are cash transactions and the money will be real, but the account will be closed before the ink is dry on the cashier's check." Max couldn't hold back his grin as Kyle nodded.

Opening the middle drawer of his desk, Kyle pulled out what was obviously a burner phone. "You'll use this to communicate with the real estate agent. Her number is already programmed in. Let me warn you, she is pushing seventy and sharp as a tack. Don't let your guard down." When Max nodded his agreement, Kyle slid the phone and a folder across the desk. "Now for the dicey part."

Jesus, you mean there's more? Hell, I'm never going to get outside to Camila.

"We were going to ask you to keep this between us. That silence applied to everyone, including Cami."

Max flinched. After the fuss he'd made about her failure to tell him she'd signed, it seemed the height of hypocritical to keep this from her.

"After what transpired a few minutes ago, I no longer

think that's a good idea. But you need to make it crystal clear the information stays between the two of you." Kyle took a drink and let out a frustrated breath before continuing. "Look, I want to talk to you about Cami."

Max already knew what was coming.

"The moment I heard the sincerity in her response, I knew it would be a mistake to continue along the same track." Max had known he was making a mistake and hoped to get things back on track as soon as possible.

"Thank fuck. I hated to lecture you like a newbie Dom, but I didn't want to stand by and watch you continue to make mistakes I know would cost you something you want so badly. Someday, you need to sit down and talk to Cam Barnes. He's had a lot of experience with D/s relationships… some good, some bad, but all of it is valuable. Let's go. I'm starving, and my sub will think I'm not coming if we don't get out there."

As they made their way through the French doors leading outside, Max felt his eyes widen. There must have been a hundred people gathered in the courtyard. Tobi spotted them and quickly made her way into her husband's arms.

"There you are, handsome. I was starting to think you'd forgotten me."

"Not in a thousand lifetimes, Kitten. Have you talked to Cami?"

"Yes. I'm not sure who had the most influence on the other. She told me more about the things she'd heard in Columbia. I'll probably have nightmares for a month. She looked at my back and that seemed to calm her a bit." Turning to Max, Tobi asked, "You want to see? I swear Ben's stitching is a work of art."

"Tobi." Kyle's growl was all the warning his wife needed. Shrugging, she gave Max a sly wink before standing on her tiptoes to kiss Kyle. Max laughed when Kyle wrapped his hands around her waist, lifting her effortlessly until their lips met.

"Just making sure we still have it, hot stuff."

"Did Ben sign off on playing tonight?" Kyle's question made Tobi's cheeks flush.

"He wants to talk to you and Kent. Something about a few restrictions. I'll bet he doesn't want you to spank me. You'll probably have to erase that tally you've been keeping. A tragic turn of events, I know. But as you always say… safety first."

Max had to cover his mouth to keep his smile from showing.

Max filled a plate and started working his way around the pool to where Camila stood talking with Enzo. Stopping several yards away, Max watched them chatting, and for the first time, he wondered what it would be like to share a woman. Could he be a part of a polyamorous relationship? It was the strangest feeling, but nothing close to jealousy. It was pure anticipation and curiosity.

"Take the chance, brother. There is nothing like knowing you've given your woman everything she didn't know she wanted. Women have at least twenty-eight erogenous zones, and you only have two hands. Those of us in poly relationships wouldn't have it any other way. Talk to Enzo. You already know he's a straight-up guy. Work with him as your third until you know if it's something that meets all your needs."

Max turned to Sage and smiled. "I hadn't considered bringing him in as a third. It would give all of us a chance to see how things are playing out."

Sage slapped Max on the back of the head with enough force to rattle his damned brain.

"Make sure you tell Jen I'm a genius. She's pissed at me right now, and I'd hate to have to paddle her pretty ass. I've got other ideas since my brother has pulled a security shift." Sage pushed his hands into his pockets and moved toward the food table. Max had seen the man eat more food than three men. *Where the holy hell did he put it?*

Max wasn't sure what was happening, but the back of his neck was suddenly tingling. Frantically scanning the area, he saw Enzo talking to Sam McCall, but Camila was no longer with him. Hurrying through the men and women congregated near the buffet, Max interrupted Enzo to ask where Camila had gone.

"She said she needed to use the powder room. Why?" The words had no sooner crossed Enzo's lips than every team member's phone buzzed with a text.

Security Breach. Front Gate. Intruder Inside Secured Perimeter. Gate Attendant needs a medic. The attached picture showed a man wearing black fatigues, a black knit mask over his face, and dark glasses.

Team members pulled weapons from hidden holsters and split up into groups. Sam and Sage pulled Jen between them before running toward the river. Max signaled Enzo to come with him as he made his way through a gate leading to the club's main room. Since Camila hadn't been at Prairie Winds long enough to become familiar with the layout, it was possible she'd have thought this was a shortcut to the women's locker room. Stepping into the dimly lit room, Max felt an unmistakable electric charge of fear in the room. He and Enzo kept their backs together as they moved in tandem, silently crossing the empty space. Nearing the short hall leading to the locker rooms, Max froze when he heard someone gasp.

"What are you doing here, Helio? How did you get in

and why are you dressed like a ninja?" Max recognized the name as the Columbian club's bartender. Their intel had listed him as someone Camila considered a friend—it looked like that was no longer the case.

"You need to come with me, Cami. The big bosses want to talk to you. Just talk. They think you took money from the bar. I tried to tell them you didn't, but they won't listen to me."

Max was stunned. If Helio thought he was going to waltz out of here with Camila, he wasn't as smart as they'd believed. When Enzo started to step past him, Max shook his head. It was important to give Camila a chance to resolve this herself. Something told Max they needed to hear what the man had to say, and he would only talk to Camila.

Chapter Twenty

Camila

IT WAS EASY to see Helio wasn't acting on his own. Cami had worked with him for two years, and in that time, he'd become one of her best friends. His movements were too hesitant to be intentional. The man didn't want to be here, making her wonder what the cartel was holding over his head.

"Talk to me, Helio. What's going on?" Cami leaned against the wall, hoping the casual pose would put the man at ease. She'd heard the shuffle of feet outside the hall and appreciated that whoever found them was giving her a moment to prove she could handle the situation.

"They promised they only wanted to talk to you. They will fire me if I do not bring you to their hotel, and I need my job, Cami."

She knew he sent money to his sister, who'd told him she used it to buy medicine for their sick grandmother. Cami also knew the sister was using the money to buy drugs because their grandmother died over a year ago. His damned sister made excuses every time he planned to visit to continue the ruse.

"What happened to the gate attendant, Helio?"

"He wouldn't let me in, so I used the hold you showed me."

Damn. She'd shown him several Krav Maga moves to help him subdue rowdy patrons without disfiguring them for life. When she took over the club, the employees were averaging three or more emergency room visits a week, and the number was even higher for customers.

"Okay. I'm glad you didn't hurt him."

"No, Miss Cami. I remembered what you said. Now, we need to go. I don't want to be fired. My grandmother needs her medicine."

Cami hated being in this position. Despite appearances, Helio wasn't a criminal. He wasn't ever going to be a rocket scientist, but neither was Cami, so who was she to judge.

"Helio, your grandmother died. Your sister has been using the money to buy drugs."

He stumbled back as if she'd slapped him. Helio's eyes filled with tears and her heart broke for him.

"Is that why Arita never lets me come visit?"

Cami nodded and wanted to kick his sister's ass for hurting him. Helio had nothing back in Columbia. He lived in a small apartment above the bar. He walked or rode the bus on the rare occasions he went anywhere other than work.

"Come on. Let's go sit down and talk, Helio. I'm hungry, and I bet you are, too." She waited a few seconds to turn and walk down the hall. The extra time would give whoever was hovering out of sight listening a chance to move. The delay also gave Helio a chance to process her words. He was a good man but didn't think fast on his feet. "Do you still enjoy mowing and flowers? I'll bet you could find a job in Texas. You don't really want to go back to Columbia and work for the cartel, do you?"

"I don't know, Miss Cami. Right now, I'm too tired to

think straight. I don't want to be in trouble for not bringing you back to the hotel. The man with the fancy suit on the plane said they needed to talk to you. Did you say there's food here?" Looking around, he smiled when he saw the bar. "This club has a big bar. Look at all those glasses. And they have pretty flowers out front, I saw them when I came in."

"Come on, this club has a nice sitting area. We'll let someone go outside and fill us a plate while we talk." She didn't want him outside in the open. Chang managed to find a sniper position once; she didn't want to tempt fate. Leading Helio to the sitting area, Camila smiled at Enzo and Max.

"Camila, Enzo, and I were on our way outside to get something to eat. Do you and your friend want anything?" Cami rattled off a list of snacks she knew Helio liked. Lilly, Dean, and Del walked through the club. Making their way over to where Cami and Helio were sitting, the Wests introduced themselves.

"Helio?" Looking from Dean to Del, Lilly laughed. "It has to be a sign. Wait until I tell Tabby. Girls trip to Monte Carlo."

Helio looked confused, and Cami understood why.

"Lilly is connecting the fact Helio Castroneves is a famous race car driver and her fascination with anything fast and explosive. The most famous race in the world, according to our beautiful wife, is in Monte Carlo."

"I know who he is. He danced with that pretty blonde girl on the dancing show. They won, too. My grandma loved that show."

Cami smiled at Helio. She'd forgotten how easy he was to impress.

"Yes, you are right. You have a good memory." Lilly's

praise made Helio's eyes shine with gratitude.

"Did I hear someone mention landscaping? If you decide to stay in Texas, you won't have any trouble finding work. Anyone here at Prairie Winds can put you in touch with us, and we'll help."

Helio was on his feet before Dean finished speaking.

"Thank you, Mr. West. You're very kind, especially since I sort of broke into your sons' place. Those fellas in suits on the plane are determined to talk to Miss Cami. They should have just called instead of dressing me up in this silly ninja costume. That Chang fella said he was going to be watching from the other side of the river to make sure I got in the boat."

The silence in the room was deafening.

Cami looked up to see Max and Enzo frozen with plates of food suspended above the coffee table. Max gave Camila a questioning look. She assured everyone Helio wouldn't lie. Hell, she wasn't sure he was capable of saying anything other than the truth. Camila learned years ago that everyone has limitations—some people are better at compensating, but we all have cognitive areas where we don't excel. Helio's challenges were simply easier to see.

Dean, Del, Max, and Enzo sprinted in different directions, causing Lilly to giggle.

"I swear the Keystone Cops could learn a thing or two from this crew when shit is hitting the fan. Oh, look, Swedish meatballs. They are my favorite. Let's eat."

Helio had been close to a meltdown a few seconds earlier. He had no idea how valuable his simple statements had been. Lilly's effortless grace made Helio relax and settle back into his seat.

"Come on Helio, you'd better grab something before Lilly and I eat everything, and we have to figure out a way to get more when everyone had to hurry off to work."

"No worries, we've got you covered." They turned to see Tabby and Tobi carrying in one of the buffet tables. Helios' eyes went impossibly wide before he rushed over to help.

"You ladies were doing fine, but my grandmother's ghost would slap me into next week if I didn't help."

Cami watched him swallow back his emotion and hated that she'd been the one to tell him about his grandmother's death. Damn, Helio's drug-addicted sister for letting him down.

"Thanks… and thanks for not hurting the fellow at the gate. I watched the replay on the security feed. Those moves were cool. I'd love to learn Krav Maga, but Kent and Kyle think I'm already dangerous enough. I want to be dangerous *on purpose*. Oddly enough, that argument seemed to make them more determined."

Tobi's smile was infectious, and Cami wanted to reach over and use her fingers to close his slack jaw. The vivacious blonde clearly had a new admirer.

"You probably bruised his ego, and his mean bosses will make him do an extra session or two of PT, but he'll be smarter next time." Lilly's observation made Helio's cheeks flush with embarrassment.

"If the men in suits hadn't made me wear these silly clothes, things would have gone better. I knew the fellow at the gate was just doing his job, but he could have called Miss Cami. She would have told the guard that I wouldn't hurt her." Helio stopped speaking to take a bite from one of the half-dozen finger sandwiches he'd piled on a small plate. Cami watched his eyes widen as he looked around. "Are you gonna work here, Miss Cami? This club is a lot nicer than the one at home."

Cami sighed. Helio wasn't going to be happy when he learned the truth, but she was tired of lying to him. Camila made a promise to herself when she signed the contract to join the Prairie Winds team—no more long-term undercover work. It was too easy to lose yourself in the process.

An hour later, Lilly, Tabby, and Tobi had engaged Helio in such a deep conversation, they'd learned more about him in sixty minutes than Cami had in two years. Kent and Kyle should recruit the trio as interrogators. As a group, they'd eaten most of the snacks on the table, and Cami felt like she could roll faster than she could walk. Leaning back, she fought the urge to close her eyes and hibernate. Damn. Maybe she'd burn off all the calories she'd consumed if she slept for a few months. She'd been eating because she was bored. Now, she dreaded the work it would take to burn off the extra calories.

"Did you miss us?" Cami launched herself off the sofa where she'd been close to dozing a few seconds earlier. "Woah. Come here, Camila." Max's voice went from teasing to concern between one breath and the next. Cami met him halfway around the expensive piece of furniture. Wrapping his arms around her, Max pulled her against his chest. Cami knew he'd feel her heart pounding as she tried to stem her fight-or-flight response to being startled. "I'm sorry, sweetheart. I didn't mean to embarrass you."

Relaxing into his warmth, Cami enjoyed being pressed so tight against him she could feel the steady beat of his heart, Cami realized how her reaction must have looked.

"I'm fine. I was fighting sleep and felt completely safe. I've felt that one other time in the past two years." Cami felt a subtle shift in his hold and pulled back so she could see his expression. "It's been hard letting go of the feeling I needed to be ready to run at a moment's notice."

"I'm pleased you feel safe here... and with me. My irritation is with myself for being so damned inconsiderate. We'd like for you to sit in on the briefing, then Enzo and I want to talk to you." He could see a spark of curiosity in her eyes. She didn't question him, simply nodded and let him lead her to Kent and Kyle's office.

Chapter Twenty-One

Cam

CAM BARNES STOOD at the head of the conference table with his arms crossed over his chest. He hadn't planned to lead this meeting, but at this point, there weren't any other viable options. Most of the Prairie Winds team already suspected his retirement was a ruse, but the next half-hour was going to remove all doubt. Damn the CIA for pulling him back into another operation.

"For the past three years, the agency I work for has been closing in on a massive criminal operation."

"Wait, did you just admit that you still work for the CIA?" Sage McCall's question wasn't about confirming what he knew... it was about forcing Cam to admit he'd been less than truthful.

Cam had known the team members would be miffed, but he was surprised the anger was surfacing this early. At this rate, it was going to be a damned long and challenging chat.

"Yes. As some of you already knew and most of you suspected, I'm still in their employ. Generally, I'm used as a resource, or I fill an advisory role. This operation was different. It has close ties to several I worked on years ago, and I have personal reasons for wanting to see them dealt with once and for all." Cam took a deep breath and looked at Carl before continuing. Carl's nod wouldn't have been noticed by anyone who didn't know him well, but the confirmation the other man had his back was reassuring.

"I lost two partners while working this case. Other operatives lost members of their families. We all lost friends and colleagues. I *retired* because they threatened to torture Cecelia and expose the members of Dark Desires. Most of the members weren't concerned with the blowback, but some were. I'd vowed to protect their privacy above all else, so as far as anyone knew, I retired."

"Over the years, your retirement became less and less convincing. I didn't know anyone at Interpol who believed it. They didn't have proof, but I did. At least, I thought I did." Cami stared at her hand as she threaded a pencil through her fingers like she had a baton as a kid. The move was self-comforting and pushed everything out of her mind except what she was trying to figure out. Cami saw Cam smile in her peripheral vision and stilled.

"Camila I'm certain you have a mountain of evidence you simply haven't put it in order yet. I have to admit I'm confused why you were interested, but I don't doubt for a minute you will be able to connect me to a dozen operations if you put your mind to it." Cam paused and grinned about her. "You are going to love working with this team. They are going to tap your brilliance and help broaden your horizons in ways you can't imagine."

Kyle cleared his throat, drawing everyone's attention before speaking.

"The attempted break-in at our home appears to have been a distraction. Facial recognition identified a trio of local vagrants with rap sheets as long as your arm. We plan to press charges to discourage them and anyone like them from being lured by cash. According to the local detective's report, they were never supposed to enter the house. They were paid to make it look like they'd become spooked before making their way inside."

"They were asked why they removed their masks when they could see the property was under video surveillance." Kent shook his head and chuckled. "These three are poster children for abstinence. They're the epitome of all the reasons drug use should be avoided at all costs. Jesus, their combined I.Q. still puts them on the short bus. With their records, they are looking at serving some serious time if they're convicted."

"Consequences." Kyle shrugged. "I'd say they should have considered the possibility before they accepted the job, but I've watched this video several times and have yet to see any spark of intelligence." Looking out one of the office windows, Kyle frowned, trying to get a better look at his mother. "What is she up to now?"

Cam watched Kent move to the window. It was easy to see when his gaze fell on their mother, who was furiously writing on a Big Chief tablet. "Is that one of those tablets kids use in primary school?"

Giving his friends a sly smile, Cam responded, "I asked about it when we were on our way in. She told me that using the rough, wide-lined paper boosted her creativity. It seems your mother has decided to take up writing. Specifically, I'm planning to write romance novels."

"What the actual fuck?" Kent shook his head and turned back to the room. "Not one word, do you understand? And I'll fire anyone who helps her." Ten seconds of absolute silence followed as Kent and Kyle stomped from the room. As soon as the door slammed behind them, the room erupted into raucous laughter.

Chapter Twenty-Two

Max

LEANING AGAINST ONE of the thick posts supporting the cabin's back porch, Max rolled the narrow neck of his beer bottle between his fingers as he watched a group of young boys trying to paddle their kayaks against the water's steady flow. They were struggling but their laughter showed how much the group was enjoying the effort.

In the three days since Chang's transfer to a federal holding facility outside Washington D.C., word filtered back to the team that he was bragging about fulfilling his contract on Tobi West. He'd misinterpreted the ambulance leaving Prairie Winds without lights and siren. After watching the compound from various locations and not seeing Tobi, Chang called his contact, requesting the balance of his fee be transferred into his offshore account. The call led investigators to his money and the man who'd hired him. As things currently stood, Chang would spend years behind bars. They still hadn't found anything to link him to any other hits, but Micah was still working on the cloned files.

"Did you change your mind?" Camila's question surprised him. He hadn't heard her enter his cabin or approach the back door. Turning to her, he smiled and shook his head as she joined him on the spacious wood-planted deck.

"No. I was just thinking about Chang and wondering if we left a stone unturned. How did your conversation with Enzo go?" After he talked to her about adding a third to their relationship, Max encouraged the two of them to talk to one another without him being involved. If this was going to work, the two of them needed time to lay a foundation of friendship.

"It was interesting. His experience in the military gives him an advantage in his work, but I think your combined experience puts me at a distinct disadvantage when it comes to anything involving sex and what I've learned is called *the lifestyle*."

Max heard the note of playfulness in her voice but suspected it was a cover. She'd stopped a little more than an arm's length from him. What was probably considered a polite distance in most social situations was unacceptable in a D/s relationship. Leaning forward, Max wrapped his hand around her wrist and tugged her forward.

"I want to be able to touch you. Have you noticed how close the submissives stand to their Doms?" It was a rhetorical question, so he was surprised when she answered.

"I have noticed but wasn't sure if it was a dynamic that developed over time or something that was expected right away. After spending most of my professional life keeping out of people's reach, it may be a hard habit to break."

"We'll work on it." Pulling her back against his chest, Max turned, so they faced the river. Gesturing to the kayaks on the river, Max said, "I've been watching them for a while. I'm impressed they haven't given up. I've only been able to catch bits and pieces of what their leader is saying, but this is clearly a lesson in perseverance. I don't know who he is, but he's doing those young men a huge favor." They watched in silence as the group slowly made their way out of sight.

Turning in his embrace, Camila laid her cheek against his chest and sighed.

"Enzo said he was joining us this evening. What are your expectations? And what are the rules? I don't want to look back on this night regretting what I didn't know."

Max understood her concern. Walking into any unknown was scary, but tonight was going to be a new level of discomfort for all of them.

"The only rule you need to remember is to follow instructions without hesitation or question. It would be a bonus if you let go of your inhibitions before we start."

"I don't have a lot of inhibitions. My parents would have had to pay attention to me in order to instill any false boundaries. And after my mom died and my dad was in prison, I became invisible. The only person who seemed to notice me was the old man across the street, the one who... Oh my lord. That's who Sam McCall sounds like. The ogre who lived across the street... the one who was always yelling at me for petting his dog when it came into our yard." Max felt her shudder at the memory. "Years later I learned he was a Vietnam War veteran with PTSD. I have always wished I'd known. I'd have tried to befriend him rather than running anytime he looked out the window."

"There are few things we need to discuss before we play." Max smiled when he saw Enzo step around the corner of his cottage.

"Do you have any physical limitations we need to be aware of? Anything preventing us from using a St. Andrew's cross, for instance?" Enzo spoke close enough to her ear Max knew she felt the warmth of his breath fan over her bare skin.

Max felt her startled reaction to the other man's proximity, but she answered without hesitation. "No."

"Blindfolds?" Max had already spoken with Enzo about Camila's hesitance entering a dark space.

"I'm not comfortable when I can't see my surroundings. When my parents found out I hid in my closet during their fights, they started locking me inside. More often than not, they forgot to let me out. It's a fear I'm working on, but I'm not there yet, so it's not a good place to start our journey."

Max agreed. He wanted to be able to look into her eyes during their scene, so blindfolds were already off the table as far as he was concerned.

"Let's move inside. I'm anxious to see Cami naked, and I'm worried about the kayaking goof troop deciding they've had enough and float back downstream." Enzo was right. They needed to move inside. No one in the world could spot a naked woman faster than a teenage boy. Their club pledges to live a wholesome life would sink like the Titanic given the opportunity to ogle a real-life woman standing in full view.

"And every one of those fellows has a cellphone. My picture would be all over the internet in less than a minute. I'm glad most of my craziness happened before phones had cameras. I shudder to think of the trouble I'd have gotten into if..."

Max smiled at Enzo over Camila's head. Damn, she was going to be fun. She'd just handed them the keys to the conversation castle. As soon as the door lock snicked behind them, Max moved behind Camila and nodded for

Enzo to begin.

"Strip, Beautiful. I want to see every inch of you." When she blinked in surprise, the other man shrugged. Moving so fast he was little more than a blur, Enzo sat in a straight-backed chair and pulled Camila over his lap. Trapping her legs with one of his, Enzo gave her ass a solid swat. "Commands are to be followed immediately unless you use your safe word. *Red* stops our play until the next day. We'll use the time to discuss what went wrong and how we can avoid making the same mistake again. I know Max has also explained you also have the option to use the word *yellow* to slow things down."

While he'd been speaking, Enzo was smoothing his hand over her barely covered ass. He suspected the short dress was the only thing she'd put on after her shower, but only time would tell. As it turned out, he didn't have to wait long for an answer. Pushing the supple fabric up until it was bunched at her waist, Enzo looked at Max and grinned.

"I love a sub who dresses for the occasion. Your ass is the prettiest thing I've ever seen." Enzo's voice was filled with appreciation, and Max agreed.

"Everything about Camila is perfection. Her mind is brilliant, her compassionate heart beats to protect those who can't take care of themselves, her heart-shaped ass is so spankable, it should be illegal... hell, her entire body is the answer to my prayers." While he'd been speaking, Camila had relaxed over Enzo's knees until he had to look closely to see if she was breathing.

"It's easy to see why you are smitten. Look at the way my handprint shows so perfectly against her flawless skin. I'm dying to know how it looks when every inch is scarlet and hot to the touch. Do you think she'll be able to come from spanking?" Enzo's question was rhetorical, so Max didn't bother to answer, but he felt his mouth twitch in amusement.

"I love hearing the way her breathing accelerates. She is a well-trained operative, but the body's autonomic responses are impossible to control when your mind is falling over the edge into a deep well of pleasure." Max wasn't sure where he was going to find the patience to stand aside and watch their third set the stage for the scene to come. Enzo smiled as he used the pad of his index finger to outline the imprint of his hand.

"One swat isn't enough for failing to follow an order. How many, little sub? Tell me what you think will take to make certain you strip on command?" Enzo's voice was almost hypnotic, but the slight shift in Camila's body language told Max she'd heard the question.

"I don't have enough experience to answer the question appropriately, Sir." She'd put just enough emphasis on the last word to let them know she was fucking with them—*silly girl.*

"There was enough sass in that answer to get her additional five. Give her ten for lack of response and five for thinking that response was appropriate." Max's words were still hanging in the air when Enzo gave Camila five sharp swats. His hand was a blur as he lit up her backside. The other man hadn't given her time to tighten the cheeks of her ass, which would have made the sensation more painful. She might not know it now, but Enzo had done her a huge favor.

"Fuck me. She took those perfectly."

Like he'd given her so much as a split second to react.

Max had to bite the insides of his cheeks to keep from laughing. Enzo's voice was filled with appreciation and wonder. The man had a dominant streak a mile wide, but Max bet Enzo would fall hard and fast when he met the right woman.

"Are you ready for the next five, Cami?" Her soft moan was the only response before Enzo rained five more swats over the crease between her ass cheeks and upper thighs. She would feel those for several hours, and the discomfort would be a good reminder of how important it was to follow instructions.

"The last five are mine." Max watched as Enzo lifted Camila to her feet, then caught her when she swayed. Sitting on the sofa, Max smiled at the dazed look in her eyes. "These last five will sting, Camila. You can come whenever you're ready." The look she gave him was impossible to misinterpret, but she'd understand soon enough. Once she was draped over his lap, Max told her to open her legs. Her full body shudder made him wonder how her body was reacting to the spanking. Sliding his fingers through her folds, he wasn't surprised at what he found. "You're soaked, little sub. Do you have any idea how much your response turns us on?"

Letting his fingers slide through the petals of her pussy, slick with her honey, Max used the tip of his index finger to draw slow circles around her swollen clit.

"Oh, God. My mind is melting."

Max was pleased to hear she was in a good place emotionally. He would continue to check in regularly, but she didn't appear to be suffering any ill effects from dealing with a second man, and she'd taken the ten swats without complaint. Leaning down, Max whispered against the sensitive shell of her ear.

"Five more. Come when you're ready." Max rubbed his hand in circles over the fleshiest part of her ass for several seconds before landing the first heated swat. He'd cupped his hand to cushion part of the intensity while increasing the sound. Max wasn't sure whether she'd gasped from the sting, or if she'd been startled by the sound. Pacing the remaining four slaps upped her anticipation and his desire. As soon as he'd given her the last swat, Max pushed his fingers into her heat, easily finding her G-spot. Pressing the pads of two fingers against the spot he knew would send her flying, Max wrapped his free arm around her waist anchoring her to his lap. The last thing he wanted was for her to buck herself off onto the hard wooden floor.

Camila's scream was music to his ears, but it was the clamping of her internal muscles that made his cock twitch against her side. Fucking hell, the woman was something else. As the slick syrup of her release flowed over his fingers, Max wished she was tied to his bed, legs spread wide as he lapped up every drop. Feeling her vaginal walls pulsing around his fingers made him ache to push his cock into the tight channel.

"Damn, watching her react to your touch was one of the hottest things I've ever seen. She took my swats like a dream, but you touched her heart." Enzo's words surprised him. "I know I can meet a specific need and add an interesting dimension to her experience, but you are the one she belongs to."

Enzo's words meant more to Max than the other man would ever know. Giving him a nod of thanks, Max picked Camila up and moved quickly to the bedroom. The two of them had already planned the scene, so there wasn't any need for chit-chat.

Seeing her sprawled in the middle of the bed, the ebony strands of her silken hair fanned over the edge of the bed, stole his breath. Max knew he would never forget this moment—whether the memory was fond or one of those he wished he could turn back time and change remained to be seen. Smiling at her soft gasp when she realized he and Enzo had removed their clothes, Max grinned as the other man tugged until her head was tipped backward over the edge of the bed.

"I'm going to fuck this pretty mouth while your Dom takes your pussy." Enzo painted the pearl of pre-cum at his tip over Camila's lips. "Spread those pretty lips for me, beautiful."

Max noted the rapid rise and fall of her breasts as her lips parted. Sliding his forearms beneath her knees, he lifted until she was perfectly positioned. At his signal, they both pushed forward. The controlled movement tested his patience more than he imagined possible.

He'd been a trained sexual Dominant since his early twenties, even working as a Dungeon Monitor at clubs near base when he'd been on leave. Max knew he needed to tap into every second of that experience to keep from plundering her. Camila was temptation personified, and for the first time in his life, Max wished he could introduce a woman to his family. She must have sensed his moment of nostalgia because she moved her hand to his, lacing their fingers together. The subtle squeeze triggered an emotion so strong, Max swore his soul was laid bare.

"Enzo's observation that you belong to me pales in comparison to the way I feel about you. I recognized your soul the moment our eyes met for the first time. Covered in dust and sweat, you were the most beautiful woman I'd ever laid eyes on. He's right, you belong to me, but I also belong to you."

Max had only pushed a couple of inches into her heat

and was already fighting the urge to thrust in until his balls were pressed against her scarlet ass cheeks. The first time he'd taken her, the sensation of his tip pressing against her cervix nearly launched him over the edge. Watching Enzo push his cock between Camila's lips was going to drive him insane. Knowing her mind was already splintering with pleasure was damned satisfying.

Camila groaned, and Max swore every muscle in her body went lax at the same time. He loved seeing her let go. Max had spoken with submissives who said their biggest challenge was letting go and allowing their mind the freedom to follow their body's needs. Before he could pull in his next breath, her vaginal walls rippled around him in ever-tightening bands.

"Fucking hell, Camila. Feeling your pussy grasp my cock, trying to hold on so I stay buried deep, is shattering my control."

"Christ almighty. You aren't the only one being tested. Her mouth is devil-blessed. The way she opens her throat for me and swallows around my cock is going to send me to heaven on a damned comet." Enzo's eyes rolled back so far, Max wondered for several seconds if the other man had been able to see behind him, but Camila's soft sighs pulled him back to the moment. When you hollow your cheeks, it feels like you're going to unravel me." Under normal circumstances, Max would have made a joke about his friend's lack of control, but he was too busy trying to manage his own restraint.

Max felt the telltale fluttering around his cock, and for the first time since he was a damned teenager, he didn't have a prayer of holding himself in check. Increasing his pace, Max was relieved to see Enzo follow his lead. As one of them pushed forward, the other pulled back, so one of them always was always buried in bliss.

Shouting her name, Max let go. Pulsing against her cervix, he felt the warmth of his release splash back against his tip and groaned. The walls of Camila's vagina tightened to the point it was almost painful. Watching Enzo throw his head back and shout for Camila to swallow every drop of the gift he was giving her was damned hot as well.

Collapsing to the side, Max was pleased he hadn't crushed her under his weight. Enzo staggered back until he fell into a chair.

"Is the top of my head still in place? I could have sworn it blew off."

Camila giggled between gasps as she tried without success to sit up.

"We need to review the plans for the annex, but my brain isn't firing on all cylinders."

"Is that what they're going to call the facility across the river?" Camila seemed mildly amused, but if she didn't have enough energy to sit up, any discussion about the blueprints spread out on his cabin's small dining room table would have to wait. At this rate, their brainstorming session wasn't going to happen until tomorrow… or maybe the next day.

Epilogue

Six Months Later

"I CAN'T BELIEVE I let you all talk me into this. I'll probably break my damned neck right in front of God and everybody. Oh, and did I mention all the people with cell phone cameras recording my tragic demise? Oh, yeah, that's an added bonus." Tobi West bounced on the balls of her feet as two men snapped the harness in place. The thick, black nylon straps were a sharp contrast to her lace-covered chiffon dress. Who knew the bride had such a girly side? If she wasn't careful, Tobi was going to moon everyone waiting in the gazebo.

"Just remember to smile as you approach the landing zone." Sage McCall grinned when Tobi gaped at him as if he'd just grown a second head. "Careful, Tobi. Just because it's a special occasion, don't think I won't throw your sweet ass under the bus."

"Snitches get stitches, Sage."

"And sassy subs get swats." The subtle shift in his tone told Tobi he was dangerously close to his tipping point. The last thing she needed was him slipping into full-Dom mode. She'd pushed as far as she dared.

She hadn't been nervous about gliding over the river to make a grand entrance until Sage's wife, Jen, let out an ear-piercing scream as she left the platform. The leggy blonde was laughing before she slid into Sam McCall's arms in the landing zone. Watching her friend glide across the open space was a treat, but Tobi set the binoculars aside and sighed.

"You know she is going to look like a blessed super-model in her pictures. The shots will end up in a bridal adventures magazine, and our girls' adventures will be ruined by fans clamoring for her autograph." Kicking a clump of grass in frustration, Tobi squeaked when the man in front of her tightened the harness to the point she had trouble pulling in a breath. "Teetering toadstools, give me a break. I need to breathe, you know. My pictures are already going to be the inspiration for Stephen King's next book. Let's not add Smurf blue to my terrorized look."

The young man blushed and muttered an apology before Sage relieved him. By the time he loosened the straps, Tobi was struggling to focus on anything other than the black dots dancing in her vision. Sage gave her shoulders a quick squeeze from behind to recenter her attention, and Tobi wondered when he'd moved.

"Go on, Sweetness. I'll be right behind you."

Sage placed her hands on handles attached to what looked like a pully, and his warm fingers gave her cold ones a quick squeeze. Before her mind caught up, he'd lifted her off the ground, and she heard the amusement in his voice when he told her to "Hang on and enjoy the ride." It took a couple of heartbeats for her to realize he'd let her go, and she was gliding over the river.

Tobi felt the grin spreading over her face as she got caught up in the joy of the moment. What on earth had she been waiting for? *This is great fun. I can't wait to tell Lilly about this.* Glancing down, Tobi sucked in a breath. *Holy hell, who blabbed? Cripes, there must be two hundred boats down there. I'll bet Micah and the rest of the men in charge of security today are crapping kittens.*

Gliding into Kyle's arms in the landing zone, Tobi knew her smile spoke volumes. Seeing Kent and Kyle waiting for her was a reminder of how much her life changed the day she met them.

"Kitten, I'm torn between being thrilled you enjoyed the zip-line and terrified we've created a monster." She started to respond, but his lips met hers in a kiss so hot, it would have melted her panties if she'd been wearing any.

"I can tell by the look on her face our wife is worried she flashed the flotilla on the river." Kent was usually tuned in to her emotions, and he was on the money today.

"It did cross my mind, but I know you wouldn't do that to me." Tobi grinned when Max landed on his feet nearby. "Dang, I would have busted my backside if you hadn't caught me. Max didn't even bounce."

"This isn't much of a challenge when you are used to fast-roping down from a helicopter with the wind and rain whipping around you."

Tobi tried not to dwell on the dangers members of the Prairie Winds team faced. Each mission was unique and tested their skills in ways she could only imagine. Max stood nearby, waiting for Camila to make her grand entrance. Tobi admired the way the two set aside traditional wedding conventions and were making the day their own.

They were suddenly inundated with hoots and hollers loud enough to wake the dead.

"Look up." Tobi followed Kent's line of sight and laughed. The three of them joined their friends, cheering loudly as Camila zip-lined across the river. Cameras flashed, and as happy as Tobi was for her new friend, a fission of fear raced up her spine at the same time.

"Are you worried about so many pictures being taken?" Kyle looked down at her and grinned. He kissed her forehead before answering.

"No, Kitten. Anyone outside the secured perimeter will find their pictures are fading as soon as they flash on the screen."

Kent leaned close, so she'd be able to hear him over the laughter. "Ian McGregor is a genius. This technology was developed in answer to music superstars' complaints about recordings of their music and their pictures being sold on the black market. In other words, they weren't getting a cut, so they were pissed. We gave it a test run a few days ago, and it didn't affect anyone inside. There are so many potential applications. This piece of technology is going to make Ian a fortune."

An hour later, Cami and Max were married. Champagne was flowing, and the party was in full swing. Tobi was listening to Lilly regaling their friends with the funny anecdotes she'd included in the first draft of her book. Lilly's publisher was thrilled with what they'd read so far, and Tobi didn't doubt the book was going to be a bestseller. A quick movement across the courtyard caught her attention, and Tobi frowned when she saw Cam move quickly into the shadows.

Tuning out everything around her, Tobi focused solely on the slender figure deep in the shadows. She was convinced it was a woman. The newcomer's silhouette was pure Jessica Rabbit, and something about the way she moved was oddly familiar.

Don't stand over there gawking. Come say hello.

"Holy crap, on a cactus in February. I can't believe it." She'd only met GiGi Stafford briefly, but Tobi felt an instant connection and knew they'd eventually be friends. Making her excuses to the ladies she'd been talking to, Tobi started across the courtyard. She'd only taken a few steps when she felt a familiar presence move in beside her. Kyle's large hand wrapped around her upper arm just above her elbow. The warmth of his palm against her bare skin was almost enough to make her veer off into a secluded space where she could have her wicked way with him.

"If GiGi is here, something's wrong. Say hello, then I'll escort you inside." Tobi didn't argue—she knew it was pointless. "They worked on a child trafficking case, and there are ties between the different groups. We suspected GiGi's cover was compromised, and her sudden appearance her this evening isn't a coincidence."

As they approached GiGi and Cam, Tobi saw a tiny flicker of light above the other woman's head. Instinctively, she launched herself at GiGi. The two of them tumbled to the ground just as a bolt of lightning pierced the ground where GiGi had been standing.

The witch looked at Tobi and laughed.

"Damn, girl, it's nice to see you again. You certainly know how to make somebody feel welcome."

The End

Books by Avery Gale

Spellbound
Spellbound – The Knights of Aradia
The Vampire's Second Chance

The Adlers
Brooklyn
London
Austin
Paris
Cleveland
Asia
Kensington
Israel
Bronx
Catalina

The ShadowDance Club
Katarina's Return – Book One
Jenna's Submission – Book Two
Rissa's Recovery – Book Three
Trace & Tori – Book Four
Reborn as Bree – Book Five
Red Clouds Dancing – Book Six
Perfect Picture – Book Seven

Club Isola
Capturing Callie – Book One
Healing Holly – Book Two
Claiming Abby – Book Three

Masters of the Prairie Winds Club
Out of the Storm
Saving Grace
Jen's Journey
Bound Treasure
Punishing for Pleasure
Accidental Trifecta
Missionary Position
Another Second Chance
Star-Crossed Miracles
Dusted Star
Lilly's Choice
Falling for Fallon
Miami Bound
Prairie Winds Pandemonium

The Wolf Pack Series
Mated – Book One
Fated Magic – Book Two
Tempted by Darkness – Book Three

The Knights of the Boardroom
Book One
Book Two
Book Three

The Morgan Brothers of Montana
Coral Hearts – Book One
Dancing with Deception – Book Two
Caged Songbird – Book Three
Game On – Book Four
Well Bred – Book Five

Mountain Mastery
Well Written
Savannah's Sentinel
Sheltering Reagan

The Christmas Painting
Taking Out the Mother of the Bride

I would love to hear from you!

Email:
avery.gale@ymail.com

Website:
www.averygale.com

Facebook:
facebook.com/avery.gale.3

Twitter:
@avery_gale